ALREADY GONE

KRISTEN PROBY

K.L. GRAYSON

Cover Designer: Kari March

Cover photo photographer: Sara Eirew

Editor: Chelle Olson

Proof reader: Tiffany Martindale

~SCARLETT~

I'M NOT GONNA LIE. I fucking love being famous. And it's not for the reasons you might think.

Don't get me wrong, the money is great. It affords me a life-style that most people pine for, and one that I never would've dreamed possible as a kid. And the perks of being a celebrity are endless. Private parties, fancy cars, more jewelry than most women could ever hope for, and A-list celebrities vying for front-row seats at my concerts. And my absolute favorite perk...award shows. There's nothing better than strutting down the red carpet in a designer gown with an equally gorgeous escort.

But here's what it all boils down to: I love fame because it was my ticket out of New Hope, South Carolina, the small town where I was born, raised, and never truly fit in. It wasn't until my boots hit the bustling streets of Nashville, Tennessee, that I felt at home.

Music brought me fame, which in turn gave me the one thing I had been searching for: an identity.

Of course, I worked my ass off to get here, and I have God-given talent that I'm eternally grateful for.

So, when I burst out on the stage in front of a hundred thousand fans who all came to scream my name, it's the thrill of a lifetime.

Every damn night.

"You're on in three," I hear in my ear. I'm in my green room alone, my hair and makeup done, and I'm wearing the first of twelve costumes for tonight. We're on the last leg of my Starlight World Tour.

This is show one hundred twenty-three of one twenty-five in four months, and I'm exhausted. My voice is tired, my body is beat, and I want nothing more than to curl up in my California king and take the longest nap on record.

But not one soul in the audience will know that tonight. I'll give them the best damn show they've ever seen in hopes that they come back for the next tour—and bring their friends.

I take a deep breath, smooth my hands down my white, off-the-shoulder T-shirt and ripped jeans held on with a few strands and a prayer, then grab my rose gold mic and hurry out to my spot under the stage.

The rest of the band is already in place, and I can hear the first few notes of one of my most popular songs, just as the stage floor opens above me, and I begin to rise onto the platform.

"Hello, L.A!" I scream, making the crowd lose their shit. For the next two hours, I work the audience, running from one end of the stage to the other, moving down the catwalk, and belting the lyrics to their favorite songs. At one point, I'm hoisted fifty feet into the air on ropes. My show is physically demanding, with no room for error.

If I screw up, I could get hurt, and I won't let that happen.

I also don't allow for any lip-syncing in my show. I sing all of my songs live, something I've always prided myself on.

After the fourth encore, I throw my hands into the air and decide to call it a night. "I love you, L.A." A thunderous roar ripples through the stadium. Chants and screams, begging me for one more song. "You're the best there is. I'll see you soon!"

I take a minute to soak in the noise, the faces, the *energy*, before running backstage to spend another two hours doing meet and greets.

This is my life, and it's amazing.

Part of it is the attention it brings. I enjoy it, and I won't apologize for it. But really, I love *everything* about my job. They want me to stand for hours meeting with fans for autographs and photos? No problem. They want me to go to hospitals to spend time with sick fans? My pleasure. Another city, another tour, another song? Whatever it takes to breathe life into what I love to do.

But it's not just the music and the notoriety, I also love the community of the country music scene. It's smaller than you'd think. The artists are brilliant, kind, and down to earth, and writing music in Nashville is every musician's dream.

And I'm living it.

I never plan to stop making music. I'll do it until I'm on my deathbed.

"Excellent show, Scar," my manager, Susan, says after the final fan leaves and I collapse in my green room, still wearing my last costume—a rhinestone-covered jacket and booty shorts over fishnet stockings—a bottle of water clutched in my hand.

"It was a fun one," I agree with a sigh. Jesus, I'm sweating. My heart is still pounding, and I'm happily exhausted. "I can't believe we only have two shows left on this tour."

"Well, we need to talk about that," Sue replies, and the concern in her eyes has me sitting up.

"What is it?"

"You need to call your sister."

I frown. "You've spoken to Alexis?"

"In the middle of *Small Town Girl*," she confirms with a nod. "I reminded her that you were on stage and promised to have you call her when all of the madness was over."

"Shit," I mutter, reaching for my phone. I'm not looking forward to this call. My younger sister isn't my biggest fan. In fact, I'm not sure she's a fan at all. We've never really gotten along, but I had hoped that would change when we became adults.

It didn't.

I moved to Nashville to pursue my career, and she stayed in New Hope, married her high school sweetheart, and had two kids. There's absolutely nothing wrong with that.

It just wasn't the path that I wanted for myself.

And Alexis has issues with that.

Here goes nothin'.

I take a long swallow of my water, then dial her number and put her on speaker. She answers on the second ring.

"'Bout time," she says.

"I just got back to the green room. What's up?"

"Daddy had a stroke."

I stand, my hand covering my mouth. "What?"

"It's not life-threatening, thank goodness, but it's bad enough that he's going to need some help for a while."

"Done. Whatever he needs. I'll hire the best," I say right away.

"Your *money* won't fix this," Alexis snaps. "Jesus, why do you always think you can put a Band-Aid on everything with your damn money?"

"Lexi, I'm saying that whatever he needs, he'll have."

"He needs you," she replies simply. "You need to come home."

"Of course, I have a few days until the next show in Nashville. I'll come home tonight, make sure he's okay, and then—"

"No, Scarlett, you need to come home to see this through. He's going to need someone with him all the time, and I have a husband and kids. For the last ten years, I've been here making sure he has everything he needs and helping to maintain the house while you've been gallivanting around the world. I'm the one who makes sure he's eating a balanced meal every night and making sure his house is clean, and the yard is maintained."

"I—"

"You jet him from state to state so he can be at your precious shows so you don't feel so guilty for not coming home, but that isn't going to fly anymore. I'm done, Scarlett. Get your ass on a plane and take some responsibility for your family."

With that, she hangs up, and my jaw opens and closes like a dying catfish.

"I've said it before, and I'll say it again. Your sister's just a joy." Sue rolls her eyes and is already tapping on her phone. "I'll cancel the last two shows and whatever interviews we have scheduled."

"No," I reply, shaking my head adamantly. "I'll go home and see him, like I said, but I'm not canceling those shows."

"Scar, your father had a *stroke* today. And as much as I don't like Alexis, this is one time that I agree with her. Go be with your family."

I get where she's coming from, I really do. And I have every intention of going home and taking care of Daddy, but this is my family, too. The band, my dancers, my back-up singers, the crew, and the fans. They've been my family for more than a decade.

I shake my head again, but Sue stands firm.

"We'll reschedule the shows for later in the summer. I've already got the crew working on getting us out of here, and I have you booked on a flight in three hours."

"I hate red-eyes," I mutter. "I'm not complaining. I know I need to get to him. Lexi didn't even let me talk to him."

The thought stops me cold.

Daddy had a stroke. Can he even talk? I've heard of stroke victims losing use of their extremities as well as their vocal ability. The severity of what's happening really hits home.

This is my daddy.

The man who played the part of mother and father. The male who learned to put my hair in pigtails because I wanted to look pretty and went without so he could afford to get me the dress I'd been dying to have.

My face must show my turmoil because Sue puts a gentle hand on my arm. "Call him," she urges me. "Your sister can't stop you from talking to him."

I nod, feeling tears prick my eyes.

"I just saw him last week. I flew him to the show in Miami."

5

"And he loved it," Sue agrees.

"Jesus, Sue. I haven't been to New Hope since I was eighteen."

"Well, I guess you're going now."

2

~TUCKER~

New Hope, South Carolina.

Population 6,129.

I know every soul represented in that number. Not a single one of them drives the shiny red Mercedes that just went speeding by.

Seventy-five in a forty-five.

I flick on my lights and press on the gas, sending my cruiser flying past the city limit sign and the godawful billboard that sits directly behind it; the one declaring New Hope home to country music superstar, Scarlett Kincaid.

It wouldn't be a big deal if this were actually her home. It's not. Scarlett may have been born here, but her fancy boots haven't landed on this soil in over a decade.

All it took was one call from a hotshot music executive to send her packing before the ink was dry on her high school diploma. Scarlett flew from this town fast enough to leave our heads spinning. Before any of us could process what had happened, little Scarlett Kincaid—the same girl who used to build forts with me in my living room while my mama made us mac 'n' cheese—had a hit single sitting at number one on the Billboard charts.

She went from homecoming queen and most likely to marry a rich spouse in our senior yearbook, to the queen of country music.

The country loves her. Hell, the whole world loves her.

New Hope...not so much. And it's high time that fucking sign comes down.

But first, I have to deal with this speed demon in the sexy red car.

I sound the sirens, and the car pulls to the side of the road and waits while I walk to the driver's side window. It's still up, the heavy tint preventing me from seeing inside. With a hand on my holster—because you never know what you're going to walk up on—I knock on the window.

The dark glass lowers.

My first thought: *this woman is absolutely gorgeous*. Long, dark hair. Pouty lips. And a tiny pink dress. Her eyes are covered by oversized aviators, but I'm sure they're as pretty as the rest of her.

My second thought: *what crazy excuse is she going to come up with to try and get out of this ticket?* It never ceases to amaze me the things women are willing to do to keep from getting into trouble. I've been offered everything from a blowjob to a pay-off to marriage.

"Do you know why I pulled you over today, ma'am?"

"Tucker?" The woman smiles, then pushes her sunglasses to the top of her head. And that's when I see the brown eyes I've spent more than a decade trying to forget. "Tucker Andrews, is that you?"

I step back and square my shoulders. "You can call me Officer Andrews. Do you know why I pulled you over today, ma'am?"

"Tucker." The woman laughs and shakes her head. "It's me, Scarlett."

At the mention of her name, I'm met with an onslaught of flashbacks. Running hand and hand through the neighborhood with her, laughing and playing, only to have her ignore me the second we got to school. The popular crowd versus the nerds who desperately tried to fit in. She the former, me the latter, and the pain it caused every time she acted as though she didn't know my name. For years, I pretended it didn't bother me because I knew that when I got home, Scarlett would meet me at the fence, and the awkwardness from the day would dissipate as though it never happened.

But it did. Day after day after day. I was a glutton for punishment. There was nothing in the world I loved more than Scarlett Kincaid, and it didn't matter how badly she hurt me, I was always willing to forgive her.

Her smile and laugh might've gotten to me in middle school and high school, but I refuse to let it affect me now.

"I know who you are."

Her smile falters. "Don't sound so excited to see me."

"Should I be? Twelve years ago, you got into your car, drove out of town, and never came back. Not a phone call. Not one single letter. Not a fucking word." She opens her mouth, probably to try and put me in my place, but I hold up a hand, stopping her. "It's funny that you showed up today because I was just thinking about you."

That has her perking up in her seat. "You were?"

I don't miss the way her eyes roam over my uniformed body. It's something I've gotten used to over the years. All of my friends filled out around their eighteenth birthday. It took me until twenty to ditch the scrawny nerd appearance and start to look more like my dad and less like…well, my mom.

The pimples disappeared, I ditched the shaggy hair, packed on about fifty pounds of muscle, added the police uniform, and the rest is history. And there's something about a man in uniform that women can't seem to resist.

That's not me being cocky, it's just the God's honest truth.

"Yup." I nod, offering her a fake smile. "I was looking at that billboard back there, the one with your face on it, wondering how hard I'd have to work to convince the city council to take it down."

"Take it down?" She shakes her head, clearly confused. "Why on earth would you want to do that?"

Resting a hand on her doorframe, I lean down. "Where's home to you?"

She furrows her brow but answers the question. "Nashville."

Point made. "That sign back there says this is your home, and since you've just stated it's not, I see no reason to keep it up. We should clear the space, allow for some other advertising to go up and draw people into the town." *And also because how in the hell am I supposed to forget how potent your smile is when I see it every goddamn day?*

Confusion and anger flash behind her eyes, and for about a millisecond, I regret my tone. Until she opens her mouth. "What did I do to piss you off?"

"Sweetheart, that list is so long, we'd never get through it."

She opens her mouth again, and for a second, I think she's going to fire off a comeback. Instead, she snaps her lips together and looks out the front windshield. "Are we done here, officer?"

"Not quite. I still have to issue you a ticket. License and registration, please."

Her head snaps toward me. "Are you serious? We're three miles from town. There isn't another car in sight."

"Doesn't matter. Law's the law, and you broke it."

Scarlett rolls her eyes. It's a gesture I often hate. But for some reason, when she does it, I find my dick getting hard, and that pisses me the fuck off.

"You were going seventy-five in a forty-five."

"Come on, Tucker," she pouts, and I know she's about to start with the plea to get out of her fine. "If I remember correctly, we broke that law every night for a week straight when you turned sixteen."

"And we got pulled over three times."

Her red lips tilt up. "But not once did we get a ticket."

"Because Officer Perry was a sick fuck and allowed the little bit of cleavage you flashed him to get us off the hook."

Scarlett's eyes flare to life. I've seen that look a thousand times, which is why I shake my head. "Don't even think about it."

"I wasn't."

Yeah, right. She thought about it, and I couldn't say that I wouldn't have enjoyed the hell out of it. "You could've killed someone."

"Tucker—"

"Or yourself. License and registration. I won't ask again," I say with an air of authority.

"For some reason, I don't think you'd care," she mumbles as she digs around in her purse and glove box. When she retrieves what she's looking for, she slaps the cards into my hand. "You're not really going to give me a ticket, are you?"

"This isn't L.A. or Nashville or New York, or wherever the hell you normally are. Your name and your money won't get you out of this."

"God," she growls, tossing her hands into the air. "I wasn't using my name or money to try and get out of anything. Why do people keep saying that?"

Instead of answering, I pat the side of her car. "Sit tight. I'll be back in a few minutes."

"I have places to be," she yells, sticking her head out the window.

"Don't we all, sweetheart?"

She huffs, and I can't help but laugh as I climb into my car. I pull up my computer, punch in a few numbers, and take a whole hell of a lot longer to go through the process of issuing a ticket than it would normally take—just to piss her off.

When the clock hits five, indicating the end of my shift, I slide from the car.

"Slow down next time," I say, handing her the ticket along with her cards.

She rips them from my hand, tosses them on the front seat, and rolls up the window without a word.

I watch her pull onto the road before climbing into my car and following behind her. Not because she's done something wrong or because I'm trying to keep an eye on her, but because I'm certain she's heading to her dad's house, and I happen to live next door.

I'm sure that'll tick her off.

I grin, enjoying myself more than I have in years.

It only takes us about ten minutes to wind our way through town. Scarlett pulls into the driveway of her childhood home, and since my brother's car is in mine, I park on the street.

My eyes are drawn to her toned legs as she climbs out of the car.

Scarlett fucking Kincaid.

If she weren't standing in front of me giving me the stink-eye, I'd swear I was seeing things.

"You didn't need to follow me home," she says, with a hand on her hip. "In case you didn't notice, I went the speed limit."

"Don't flatter yourself. I wasn't following you."

"Really?" She lifts a well-manicured eyebrow and crosses her arms over her chest.

She's as untouchable now as the day she left.

"You haven't changed a bit," I say, leaning a hip against the back of my car.

"What's that supposed to mean?"

"Nothing." Fighting a grin, I shake my head and walk up my driveway toward the house at the same time my brother steps onto the front porch.

"I don't have time for this shit. I'm going in to see my dad." She grabs something from her car, locks it, and heads for the front door.

"You're heading in the wrong direction."

She stops, her purse clenched tightly in her fist. "Excuse me?"

"Your dad's not here. He had a stroke yesterday."

"Yes, I know. Why do you think I'm here?"

I want nothing more than to make some offhanded comment about her being so disconnected from her family and the life she left behind that she doesn't even know where her own father is, but the thought of Rick lying in a hospital bed waiting to see his little girl stops me.

Richard Kincaid is one of the best men I know, and it's not his fault that his daughter is a selfish brat.

"He's at New Hope General. He's getting released after the doctor makes evening rounds."

Scarlett lifts her eyes as though she's shocked that I know more about her dad's whereabouts than she does. Or maybe it's disappointment. Who the hell knows?

"How do you know he's getting released?"

"Lexi called me."

"Lexi," she laughs. "Since when do you call her *Lexi*? You used to hate my sister."

"You've been gone a long time. A lot has changed." Stuffing my hands into my pockets, I turn toward my house. "Welcome home, princess."

3

~ S C A R L E T T ~

"WELCOME HOME, PRINCESS," I mimic as I drive my car—faster than the speed limit, thank you very much—and wish that I'd taken up smoking in the eleventh grade when Sheila Masters tried to push a cigarette on me.

Because I'm mad, and it's too damn early to drink.

Not to mention, I gave that up a long time ago.

Who the hell does Tucker Andrews think he is speaking to me like that? I was never anything but nice to that guy. I mean, was a warm hello too much to ask for after being gone so long?

Apparently so. If this is how my return to New Hope is going to go, I'll be escaping back to Nashville as soon as humanly possible. Even if I have to pack up Daddy and take him with me.

I park my rental and hurry into the small hospital where I was born. A young woman at the visitor desk looks up at me with a smile, and then her eyes widen, and she blinks rapidly.

"Holy shit," she says.

"Hi," I reply and flash her a smile in return. "I'm here to see Rick Kincaid. Can you please tell me what room he's in?"

"They told me you might visit," she says, swallowing hard. "But I wasn't prepared."

"Well, I'm his daughter." I wink at her and keep the grin on my face, but I want to shake her. *Just tell me where he is!*

"Of course," she says, clearing her throat as she types on her keyboard. "You know, I'm a singer."

Of course, you are. I refrain from rolling my eyes, but just barely.

"That's awesome."

"I put some videos on YouTube. My name is Kathleen Perry. Maybe you could go listen sometime. I've sung some of your songs."

"Thank you," I reply. "I'll be sure to do that. But could you please tell me where I can find my daddy?"

"Oh, I'm sorry," she says with a giggle. "I got carried away. Your dad's in room three twelve. Take the elevator to the third floor and make a right."

"Great, thank you."

I hurry away before I get sucked into more conversation. She's a nice woman, but I'm anxious to see my dad.

The elevator takes forever to arrive, and I can feel her eyes on my back, so I rush over to the stairwell and climb the three flights, taking two steps at a time. I'm not even breathing hard when I rush through the doors on the third floor and find the room.

"There's my girl," Dad says when I come through the door.

"Hi, Daddy." I rush over to him and kiss his cheek, then park my hip on the bed next to him. He looks pale and tired, but his speech doesn't seem affected, and that's a wonderful thing. "How are you feeling?"

"Oh, I'm fine, honey. I keep telling everyone that I'm fine, but they don't listen."

"Because you'd never say if you weren't," I remind him and look over at Alexis, who's sitting on the windowsill, her hands in her lap, and her mouth locked shut. "Hey, Lexi."

"Took you long enough to get here," is all she says.

"I had to take a red-eye to Charleston, then rent a car and drive down. You know it's not easy getting in or out of here."

She doesn't reply, just narrows her eyes and glares at me.

Typical Alexis.

"I'm happy to see you," Dad says and kisses my cheek.

"I'm happy to see you, too," I reply with a smile. "When can we spring you out of here?"

"Soon, I hope," he says and sighs.

"Dad, you had a stroke," Lexi reminds him.

"Tell me everything," I say. "Lexi didn't tell me much last night."

"We were having dinner," Dad begins, frowning. "I was at Lexi's place, and she made us spaghetti."

"Yum," I say with a smile, but Lexi just rolls her eyes.

"Suddenly, I was having trouble chewing and talking, and then my face started to feel funny. Thankfully, Jason was there, and he called an ambulance right away."

Lexi's husband, Jason, is a family doctor in New Hope.

"Thank goodness," I agree and smile as I brush my fingers through my dad's salt and pepper strands. He's sixty, but he still has a full head of hair.

"He had a hemorrhagic stroke," Lexi explains. "They caught it early enough and were able to administer medicine to keep it from getting worse. He's had scans and bloodwork and, thankfully, everything seems to be stable right now."

"Do they know what caused it?"

"High blood pressure," she says, giving Daddy a pointed look.

"I didn't know you had high blood pressure."

He shrugs as though it isn't a big deal. "The doctor may have mentioned it a time or two."

"And you didn't think you should do something about it?"

Dad stares at me and then looks at Alexis for help. When he realizes that she's not going to take his side, he sighs. "I know, okay? I know. I shouldn't have ignored it."

Lexi clears her throat and takes a step forward. "They started him on blood pressure medicine, but the damage has already been done. He has right-sided weakness and will require occupational, speech, and physical therapy."

"You have some work to do," I say to him and kiss his forehead. "But if anyone can do it, it's you, Daddy."

"I'll be fine," he says again.

"I'm staying with you," I say, surprising us all. Now that I'm here, and I see Dad like this, there's no way I can entertain leaving anytime soon. I need to be here for him, to make sure he's okay. And not because Lexi threw one of her fits.

Because I love him, and I *want* to be here with him through this.

"You don't have to do that," Dad says, but I'm already shaking my head.

"Yes, I do. Dad, you need someone to take you to and from therapy and to help you out at home. I know Lexi's awesome, but she has kids and her own household to run."

"I'll be fine by myself," he says, but he doesn't sound so sure.

"It's already been decided," I reply, standing to put my hands on my hips. "I'm here indefinitely. We get to be roomies again."

"Well, this is a treat," he says with a laugh.

"I don't know how to cook very well," I warn him with a smile. "But I'm sure Lexi can give me pointers."

"Sure, she will," Dad says, and we both look over at Lexi, who looks like she's about to explode into a trillion pieces. "Lexi?"

"Sure," she says with a huff. "Scarlett just waltzes in here and saves the day, but *I'm* still the one who gets to do everything."

"You know what?" I reply, not letting my smile slip even though she's hurting my feelings. She always does. I should be used to it by now. "Don't worry about it. I'll grab some recipes from the internet. Dad and I won't starve."

She sighs, looking a little guilty, but she won't look me in the eyes, and I know damn well that I'll never get an apology from her.

"I'll bring over some things you can freeze and just warm up," she says to Dad. "It'll be okay."

"Thank you," Dad replies. "Now, where is that doctor? I'm ready to go home. *The Bachelor* is on tonight."

DADDY WASN'T LYING. He totally watches *The Bachelor*. And, it seems every other reality TV show there is because he told me his whole TV schedule on our drive home from the hospital.

"How's it going?" Sue asks in my ear.

"Not as bad as I thought," I reply, sitting on the full-sized bed in my old bedroom. "Dad's downstairs watching TV. I have all of his medicines, and a schedule of therapies to take him to. He can walk, but he's shaky, so he needs a walker to start off with, and my dad is as stubborn as they come, so he's not happy about it."

"But he's going to be okay?"

"Yes," I reply confidently. "He's going to recover. It's just going to take a little time."

"I'm glad you're there, Scar."

"Honestly, I am, too. Lexi's fit to be tied, and Tucker's not happy to see me, but Dad is, and I'm here for him."

"Who's Tucker?"

The best friend I ever had who now doesn't even want to look at me.

"A guy I used to know. He pulled me over on my way into town."

I tell Sue the story, and she immediately laughs.

"Okay, so it's funny now, but it wasn't then."

"I'm just glad you're there safe and sound, and that Rick's going to be okay."

"Me, too."

"Now, what do you need?"

I stare around the room, suddenly feeling a little lost. My dad's house has been updated. Last year, he called to let me know that he needed some new plumbing and electrical work, and I took the opportunity to remodel a bit. So, the house is comfortable, and we shouldn't have any issues there.

"I don't think I need anything right away," I reply, thinking about it. "I have a lot of clothes with me. I brought my laptop and guitar so I can write. Oh, I know."

"Name it."

"I rented a car in Charleston, but since I'm here indefinitely, I'm going to need a more permanent mode of transportation. I'll see if Dad will let me drive his around since he won't be cleared for driving for a while."

"Want me to arrange for the rental company to come and get the car?"

"Yeah." I sigh and rub my hand over my eyes. Shit, I'm tired. "Thanks. Thanks for everything, Sue."

"Hey, this is what I do, remember?"

"You're good at it."

"I know." I can hear the smile in her voice. "Don't worry about anything at all. Go take care of your dad, and just holler if you need me."

"Will do."

We hang up, and I sigh again. My room hasn't changed since I left town. My old cheerleading uniform still hangs in the closet, my homecoming queen tiara rests on a shelf, and there's even makeup sitting on the vanity.

A photo tucked in the corner of my mirror catches my attention. I walk over to get a closer look. When I realize it's a picture of Tucker and me, I pick it up. A thick coat of dust hides Tucker's wide smile. Using my thumb, I wipe it away, remembering the day the photo was taken. Daddy took us fishing at old man Langerman's pond. I caught a fish on my first cast. Tucker wrapped his arm around my shoulders, congratulating me at the same time Daddy captured the moment.

With a smile tugging at the corner of my mouth, I tuck the photo back where it was and blow out a long breath. I wasn't expecting to see that. Hell, I wasn't expecting to see any of this.

It's as if I took a short trip, and Dad expected me to come right back.

Maybe he had, preparing for if the Nashville thing didn't work out.

I shake my head and decide to leave my past in the past for now. After checking the bathroom for towels, I pull fresh sheets out of a closet and dress the bed.

Once that's finished, I walk down to find Dad asleep in front of the TV. His arms are crossed over his chest, and he's snoring softly.

My God, what would I have done if this hadn't been a little stroke? What if I'd lost him?

The enormity of the last twenty-four hours hits me, and I just hang my head in my hands and let the tears come.

"Hey, baby girl, what's wrong?"

I look up in surprise and wipe the tears from my cheeks.

"You were sleeping."

"Nah, I was just resting my eyes," he says with a wink. We both know that's a little white lie.

"I guess I'm just tired," I say and then sigh and sit next to him on the couch, holding his hand, noting his weak grip. "Everything just kind of hit me."

"It's been a busy day," he agrees. "Thank you, Scar. For being here."

"Nowhere else I'd rather be," I remind him. "But if you wanted me to come home, you could have just asked. This seems a bit dramatic."

He chuckles and tries to squeeze my hand. "I'll remember that next time."

4

~ TUCKER ~

"You didn't ID her."

"Didn't need to," Scooter says, grinning as he watches the young blonde strut away.

My cousin is nothing if not a ladies' man. He has more charm in his pinky than most men have period. The problem is, he doesn't know when to shut it off, and his boyish grin has gotten him into trouble more than once.

"Damn it, Scooter. I'm off duty tonight. The last thing I want to do is watch another officer haul you off to jail."

"No, the last thing you want to do is bail me out."

"That, too." I don't smile back at him when he tries to use his charm on me.

"Well, don't worry about either one of those. She's over twenty-one."

"How do you know? You didn't even card her."

"The same way I know about the birthmark on her right inner thigh, and how I know she likes to scream out that I'm her *Big Daddy* when she's about to—"

I hold up my hand. "I get it. You've slept with her."

He shrugs. "Once or twice. And you know I don't dip my stick into just anyone. I have standards."

"Jesus." Shaking my head, I take a drink of my beer. Sure, he has standards. Those of an alley cat.

"And for the record," he adds, "I carded her when she first came in."

"Thank God."

"Have some faith in me, *officer*." I flip Scooter the bird, and he lifts a brow. "You are a ray of fucking sunshine tonight. What's gotten into you?"

"Not a damn thing."

"Scooter, beer, now," my brother says, sitting on a stool beside me. Scooter slides a draft across the bar, and Dean picks it up. "Where's Chloe?"

"Sleepover with a friend."

He nods. "You're drinking tonight, I see."

"One or two."

"One-word answers. Who pissed in your Cheerios?"

"No one. Christ, what is up with you two tonight?"

Dean looks, and Scooter quickly waves him off. "Don't worry, he's just PMSing. I'm pretty sure our boy Tucker grew a vagina. That's the only explanation I've got for the grumpy mood."

I flick the cardboard coaster at Scooter's head. He chuckles at my failed attempt and sets another on the bar top for me to use. I consider leaving the rest of my beer and heading home. A quiet night to myself sounds pretty damn good right about now, but there's no way these two fuckers will let me get away with that.

Not when they can already tell that something is bothering me.

Well, not something. Some*one*.

Dean and I grew up with our cousin, Scooter. We were all close in age, and with our mothers being twins, we spent the majority of our childhood together. Which means, my brother and cousin are overprotective and nosy as hell, and if I leave now, one of them will likely follow.

"Your bad mood doesn't have to do with Scarlett being back in town, does it?" Dean guesses, and I narrow my eyes at him while

I take another sip of my beer. Shit, this might be the first time in years that I decide to have more than two drinks. I have Scarlett to thank for that.

"Wait." Scooter stands up straight, a wicked gleam in his eye. "Scarlett is home?"

I tip back my head and finish off my beer. "Yup."

"Scarlett Kincaid?" he clarifies.

"The one and only."

"No shit?"

"She got back a few days ago," Dean offers.

"She still hot?"

"Can we not fuckin' talk about her?"

Someone must walk through the front door of the bar because I feel a gush of warm air, but I don't turn to see who it is. Instead, I slide my glass to Scooter.

"One more."

He ignores my request as his eyes lock on something over my shoulder. "Oh, yeah, she's totally hot."

"I said I'm not talkin' about it."

"You don't need to. I've got a front-row seat."

Dean and I whip around and, sure as shit, there she is in pink cotton shorts and a white tank top, looking nothing like the woman she's become and everything like the girl she used to be. Her dark hair is a wild mess on top of her head, and there isn't a lick of makeup on her gorgeous face. She's never looked as beautiful as she does right now.

I scowl as I shift in my seat, my dick twitching at the sight of her.

Down, boy.

"What the fuck is she doing here?" I grumble.

"Well, well, well. If it isn't little Scarlett Kincaid." Scooter lays the charm on thick, and she answers with a blinding-white smile. "Welcome to Scooter's," he says, rounding the end of the bar.

"Scooter Bennett." Scarlett giggles when he wraps her in a giant hug. "Well, aren't you a sight for sore eyes?"

23

"Did you hear that, everybody?" he yells, garnering the attention of everyone in the room. "Scarlett Kincaid loves me. We're getting married."

She swats playfully at his chest and pushes him away. "You haven't changed a bit."

"Neither have you, darlin'." He gives her a kiss on the cheek and takes his place back behind the bar.

"When did you do all of this?" she says, looking around the tavern.

I turn around, trying to take in the place through the eyes of a newbie. Scooter's is like a second home to me. Hell, my daughter practically lived here when we gutted the place.

Exposed wood beams run the length of the ceiling. The hardwood floors are scuffed and worn, a testament to the number of people who have enjoyed a twirl around the dance floor. High-top tables and a few booths are scattered along the walls. A stage, which boasts a live band on any given Friday and Saturday night, is tucked in the corner. A small billiard room sits off to the right, and my favorite part about this place, the kitchen, is situated behind the bar.

You won't find a better piece of apple pie than the one Scooter serves.

"We remodeled a few years ago." He pats the bar top. "It's my baby."

"This is wonderful, Scooter. I'm real proud of you." Scarlett turns toward the bar and has no choice but to acknowledge me. "Hey, Tuck. Dean," she adds, tipping her head at my brother.

He tilts his beer in her direction. "How are ya, Scarlett?"

"I'm doing good. Thank you for asking."

"What can I get ya to drink?" Scooter asks, grabbing a glass from under the bar.

"Oh, I'm not here to drink. I called in a to-go order of food with the kitchen."

"Let me go see if it's ready."

Scooter disappears, and Dean clears his throat. "So, uh, how's your dad?"

"He's good. Came home two days ago."

"Is he waiting in the car?" I ask, ready to go out and talk to him if he is. I haven't seen Rick since his stroke.

"Oh, no. He's at home."

I furrow my brow. "Is Lexi with him?"

"No." Her eyes dart to Dean and then back to me. "Is she supposed to be?"

"Are you fuckin' kidding me? You left him at home by himself?" My harsh words echo through the bar, and a hush falls over the small crowd.

"For five minutes. He'll be fine." The flippant tone of her voice only fuels my anger.

"He had a stroke, Scarlett. What if he tries to get up and falls?"

"I told him not to get up until I get back." She props her hand on her hip, lifts her chin, and pins me with those defiant eyes of hers.

I laugh humorlessly. "And you think he's going to listen?"

"Of course, he will."

"You're a piece of work, and you're the one who hasn't changed a bit. You don't think about anyone but yourself."

"Fuck you, Tucker."

"There's not enough alcohol in this bar to make that happen."

Dean stands up and puts a hand on my shoulder. "Calm down, brother."

I easily shake him off. "Do you even know your father? He's more stubborn than you are. He thinks he's fine and doesn't need anyone to stay with him, and you think that just because you told him to sit tight, he actually will?"

Scarlett's lips part, no doubt to give me a piece of her mind, but nothing comes out. Her face pales, and next thing I know she's running out the front door mumbling something that sounds an awful lot like *shit, he's totally right.*

"Two spaghetti dinners and an extra side of garlic—" Scooter's words cut off when he notices that Scarlett is gone. "Where'd she go?"

"Loverboy here just made the poor girl cry."

I shoot Dean a look. "She did not cry."

"Maybe not, but you were an ass."

"She left Rick home by himself," I argue.

"Well, congratulations." Scooter sets the bags of food on the bar in front of me. "You just bought two spaghetti dinners and a side of garlic bread. That'll be eighteen fifty."

Rolling my eyes, I pull my wallet from my back pocket and slap two tens on the bar. "Your spaghetti is overpriced."

"And you're a shitty tipper." He snags the money and shoves it into the cash drawer. "Now, get outta here and take that poor girl and her dad their food."

"Poor girl, my ass," I mumble. Grabbing the bags, I turn for the door. "You're dead to me, Scooter. You too, Dean," I say when he snickers.

Scooter just laughs. "We still on for Sunday dinner?"

"Yeah, yeah. See ya then."

"Good. And, Tuck," he yells, when I kick open the front door. "Pull that stick outta your ass before you knock on her door."

By the time I make the short drive home, my anger subsides, and I almost feel bad for the way I talked to Scarlett. Rather than pull into Rick's driveway, I park in mine and walk across the front yard, which is overgrown. I make a mental note to get it mowed sometime this week.

With a deep breath, I climb up the steps toward the front door. The house is quiet aside from the murmur of the television wafting through an open window. With the bags hanging from one hand, I use the other to knock.

"No, you stay put," I hear Scarlett say.

The sound of the television is muted, and a second later, the door flings open. Scarlett stands in the doorway, and she looks pissed.

Or maybe hurt.

A pang of guilt hits the center of my chest.

"What do *you* want?"

I hold out the bags of takeout. "You forgot your food."

She seems shocked that I'd take the time to bring it to her. She stares at the bags for a few seconds and then yanks them from my hand and slams the door in my face.

Okay, I probably deserved that.

I'm still processing what just happened when the door whips back open.

"Here." Scarlett holds out some money. "I forgot to pay for the food before I left."

"Don't worry about it, I've got it covered."

"Take the damn money." She tries to shove it against my chest, but I step back, preventing her.

"I don't want your money, Scarlett."

"Well, I don't want to owe you, *Tucker*." I'm quick. She's quicker. In the blink of an eye, she has the wad of money shoved into the breast pocket of my shirt, and the front door slams in my face.

Again.

Damn, she's feisty.

Stunned, I run a hand along the back of my neck and debate whether to knock or say "fuck it" and go home.

Home would be the easy choice.

But she deserves an apology.

I've been in a shitty mood since she arrived back in town, and it has nothing to do with the woman herself and everything to do with the feelings I harbor for her. Feelings I thought were long gone. Feelings I damn sure don't want to have.

For the third time tonight, her front door flies open. "What's your problem, Tucker?"

"You," I blurt, startling us both. There's silence for a heartbeat as we just stare at each other.

"Me?"

I've already admitted it, there's no sense turning back now. "Yup."

"But I haven't even been home. What could I have possibly done to make you mad?"

"That's exactly the point. You haven't been home. *For twelve fucking years.* You're so goddamn selfish. You just up and left your friends, your family. Everyone. And you never looked back. Not once."

"Hold grudges much?" But it's not bitchy. In fact, she looks completely flummoxed.

"I'm not holding a fucking grudge, Scarlett. I'm hurt."

Good Lord, Scooter is right. I grew a fucking vagina, and now I sound like a pussy.

Scarlett's eyes widen and then soften at my admission. "Tucker—"

"Tucker, is that you?" Rick sidles up next to Scarlett and pokes his head out the door.

"Daddy! What are you doing up? You know you're not supposed to get up on your own." She looks at me with wide, pleading eyes. "Can you keep an eye on him for one second while I grab his walker?"

"Sure."

I step forward. With one hand against Rick's back and the other on his arm, I make sure he's steady.

"You here to ask my little girl on a date?"

I nearly choke on my saliva. "No, sir. I just stopped by to drop off the spaghetti."

"Oh." He frowns. "Well, that's too bad. Scarlett could use a good, strong man like you in her life."

Scarlett shows up a few seconds later with the walker. "I don't need a man, Daddy. Quit trying to pawn me off."

"If you don't need a man, then I don't need this damn thing."

"Yes, you do," she admonishes. "Your physical therapist and occupational therapist said you need to use the walker until you regain the strength in your arm and leg."

Rick looks at me and rolls his eyes before skirting off toward the living room. "Come on in and have some spaghetti with us," he hollers. "We can talk about the date you're going to take her on."

"Daddy, Tucker and I are not going on a date."

"Sure, ya will. Just as soon as ya both pull your heads outta your asses."

Scarlett closes her eyes and fights a smile. When she looks up, I feel it like a punch to the gut. "Sorry about that."

"It's okay."

"I, uh...I'm gonna go eat before the food gets cold."

"Yeah." I glance over at my house and then take a step back. "I need to get home anyway. It's been a long day."

She nods, and I turn on my heel. I'm halfway down her walk when Scarlett calls out to me.

"Tuck?"

"Yeah?" I glance at her over my shoulder.

"Thanks for bringing the food over."

"You're welcome, princess."

Her easy smile falls. "Quit calling me that."

"Call it like I see it."

I expect some sort of quick retort. Instead, Scarlett growls and slams the door.

5

~ TUCKER ~

"Hey, sweetheart. How was your sleepover?" I grab Chloe's bag from her hand and wave to Jessica's dad as he pulls out of the driveway.

"We had fun."

"What'd you do?"

She shrugs. "Stuff."

"Stuff. That's it? What kind of stuff?"

"Just...girl stuff."

Okay. This conversation is going nowhere fast. "What do you want to do today?"

"Can I play on my iPad?"

"Twenty minutes. It's nice outside, and you're not going to waste your Saturday staring at a screen."

"None of my friends' parents limit their electronic time."

"You'll thank me later."

"Probably not." Chloe grabs her iPad and curls up in the corner of the couch.

My little girl is growing up so fast. Long gone are the days of her following me around the house, begging to play dolls or have a tea party. There's no more water gun fights or digging in the mud. These days, she's all about her friends and clothes and makeup—which I refuse to let her wear. Maybe when she's twenty we'll talk about it, but eleven is way too young, and I don't give a shit what other girls in her class are doing.

What I wouldn't give to rewind time and relive the earlier days of her childhood. The ones where she didn't back-talk or roll her eyes. The ones where I was her hero and could do no wrong.

Everyone told me to enjoy it while it lasted. At the time, I thought they were crazy. How in the hell was I supposed to enjoy fatherhood? It was never-ending: the sleepless nights, crying, bottles, and an endless number of poopy diapers. Oftentimes, I walked through life like a zombie, praying that I'd get more than four or five hours of sleep. So, yeah, at the time, I wasn't enjoying parenthood.

But I was also a single father working a full-time job and taking care of a house entirely by myself. It was exhausting. Still is, albeit a little easier without a tiny rug rat attached to my ankle.

Hindsight is twenty-twenty, and I see now what everyone was talking about.

"Hey, Chlo?"

She doesn't even look up. "Yeah?"

"Do you wanna shoot some hoops?"

"Nah."

"We could have a water gun fight. I've got those old Super Soakers in the garage."

"I'm good."

"Afraid you'll lose to your old man?"

Chloe finally glances up. She looks so much like her mother that I sometimes have to blink to remind myself that it's not Valerie sitting there. "Dad, I just wanna watch this YouTube video."

Damn. "Okay. I'm going to be outside."

"Okay, Dad."

I'M JUST FINISHING up changing the oil in my truck when I hear a muted curse. I grab a towel from my workbench and walk outside in time to see Scarlett kick her dad's lawnmower.

"Stupid piece of shit."

"Everything okay over there?"

Scarlett looks up. She blows a chunk of hair out of her eyes and waves me off. "Fine. Everything's fine."

This is going to be entertaining. I grab a lawn chair from the garage and park my ass in the middle of the driveway.

When Scarlett sees me sitting there, she stops fussing with the mower and glares at me. "What're you doing?"

"Watching you."

"This isn't a fucking show, Tucker. Go back to whatever it is you were doing."

"I'm done doing what I was doing. Now, I'm watching you."

My words prompt her to flip me the bird. "I hate you, Tucker Andrews."

"The feeling is quite mutual," I lie.

Because I don't hate Scarlett Kincaid. Not one bit. I sure as hell wish I did because it would make things a lot easier. But after lying in bed awake half the night thinking about her, I realized one thing; despite all the anger I've carried around, my feelings for her haven't changed. She's still the prettiest girl I've ever seen. She still drives me absolutely crazy. And she knows how to press every button I have. I'm utterly and completely smitten by the girl, attitude and all.

And for the first time in twelve years, I find myself smiling for no reason.

"What the hell are you smilin' at?" she huffs.

"You. You make me smile."

That has her standing up straight. "Are you drunk?"

"Nope."

"High?"

I laugh. "I wish."

Scarlett just shakes her head and goes back to the lawnmower.

I could tell her that it's not starting because it's out of gas, but what would be the fun in that? I'm actually kind of glad I forgot to fill it back up after I mowed Rick's lawn two weeks ago.

It won't hurt her to figure something like that out on her own. I bet Scarlett hasn't mowed a lawn since she was seventeen. If I had to guess, I'd say there's a lot of things she hasn't done, like go grocery shopping, change a light bulb, clean out a drain, or plunge a toilet.

Yeah, I'm totally not telling her it's out of gas.

I kick my legs out in front of me and relax in my chair, content to sit there and watch her figure out what the problem is.

She pushes on the choke several times and tries to start it. Nothing. She flips the lawnmower over and meticulously cleans out every blade of grass from underneath and then tries to start it again. Nothing. I choke back a laugh when she digs out the manual and tries to troubleshoot it that way. Nothing.

After thirty minutes of failed attempts, Scarlett puts her hands on her hips and marches toward me.

"Well, are you going to help me or not?"

"I've just been waiting for you to ask."

She gives me a *well* look.

"What's the magic word?"

She growls. "You drive me insane."

I grin. "Nope, that's not it. Let me give you a hint. It's one word. Chloe has been using it since she was two, so I'm confident you can, too."

"Please," she says between gritted teeth.

I push up from my chair and walk across the yard. "I would love to help you out, Scarlett. Why did you wait so long to ask?"

She grumbles something as she follows behind me. I grab a gas can from the garage, fill up the lawnmower, and start it on the first pull.

"Voila."

Scarlett's jaw drops. "That's it? It just needed gas?"

"Yup."

"Why do I feel like you knew that all along?"

"Because I did."

"Dad!"

Scarlett and I turn at the sound of Chloe's voice. She's standing at my back door, looking toward the garage.

"Over here, Chlo," I holler.

Chloe swivels around and darts across the yard barefoot then skids to a halt a few feet in front of us. "Can I please have more time on the iPad? I promise I won't—*whoa*. You're..." Chloe blinks several times. Her eyes dart to mine and then back to Scarlett. "I... I can't believe it...You're..."

"Chloe." I swat her arm. "You're being rude."

"Dad, that's Scarlett Kincaid."

"Yeah, I know."

"*The* Scarlett Kincaid."

"I'm sorry about Chloe," I whisper to Scarlett, embarrassed. "She's normally not like this."

"It's okay." Scarlett wipes her hand off on her shirt and holds it out to Chloe. "It's nice to meet you."

Chloe's jaw hangs open as she clasps her hand around Scarlett's. "It's nice to meet you, too. I'm a huge fan. Like a *huge* fan. My dad has told me so much about you."

Scarlett lifts a brow and looks at me. "He has?"

"She means *your* dad."

"No, I don't." Chloe shakes her head, drops Scarlett's hand, and looks at me. "You told me all about her." She turns her attention back on Scarlett. "He said you were his best friend and that he knew you'd be a star one day. 'She was born for it,' isn't that what you said, Dad?"

Scarlett's eyes search mine, looking for the truth, and I feel my cheeks heat.

"Your dad talks about you all the time, too," Chloe says, continuing her one-sided conversation. "He's so proud of you. Sometimes, we just sit and listen to your music. He knows every song of yours word for word, just like me. And a few months ago, he let me play that old guitar that's under your bed."

Scarlett's head whips toward Chloe, and I'm thankful for the momentary reprieve of her knowing gaze. "He still has that?"

"Oh, yeah. And it's in perfect shape. Rick cleans it regularly and makes sure all the strings are in good condition. He's even had it tuned a few times."

"Why would he do that?" Scarlett asks softly, although I'm certain her words weren't meant to be said out loud. Chloe answers anyway.

"Because he was waiting for you to come home."

"He...what?"

"Well, he didn't say that exactly, but that's the vibe I got. He wanted to make sure it was ready for you when you came home."

Scarlett blinks and looks down at the ground. There's a long pause, and then she glances up. Her wide, brown eyes are swimming with tears. "And I never did."

"Chloe, can you go inside and...do something?" I ask.

"Do what?"

"I don't care. Something. Wash your hair."

"But my hair is clean."

"Do your homework."

"It's Saturday."

"Chloe," I snap.

She holds up her hands. "Okay, okay. I'm going."

I wait until she's out of earshot to turn to Scarlett. A tear trickles down her cheek, and I fight the urge to wipe it away.

"You were right." Her voice cracks. "I was selfish. I *am* selfish. I left without a second thought and broke my daddy's heart."

"Scarlett—"

She shakes her head and swallows. "Please, don't. Don't try to justify my actions."

"I wasn't going to."

"Good." She brushes away the tears and looks up. "I'm gonna go in and get cleaned up."

"Okay."

She steps away, and I reach for the lawnmower.

"You don't have to do that. I'll finish it later. Just not right now. I need a minute to myself."

"I don't mind. Go take a shower and relax. I've got this."

Her bottom lip quivers, and she nods before slipping into the house.

It only takes about twenty minutes to mow Rick's lawn, and then another ten to weed-eat. When I'm finished, I top both tools off with gas and make sure they're ready to use next time. When I'm stepping out of the garage, I notice Scarlett standing by her dad's back door.

Her wet hair hangs over her shoulders. Her eyes aren't red or puffy, but they hold a sadness that tugs at my heart.

"The yard is good for at least another two weeks."

"Thanks."

"You're welcome."

"Hey, Tucker?"

"Yeah?"

"Would you and Chloe like to come over for dinner tonight? I'm cooking."

"You?" I fight back a grin and expect a smart-ass comment, but it never comes. Instead, Scarlett's back stiffens, and she crosses her arms over her chest. "I'm sorry, I didn't mean—"

"Six o'clock. Come or don't come. I don't care either way."

She darts back inside before I have a chance to tell her we'll be there.

***

"THAT WAS AMAZING." I wad up my napkin and toss it on the plate. "I'm stuffed."

"You did a wonderful job, sweetheart," Rick says, rubbing his belly. "And you didn't even burn the house down."

Scarlett chucks her napkin at her dad, and we all laugh.

"What's for dessert?" Chloe asks.

"Chloe—"

"What? Like you weren't thinking it."

I give her a pointed look. She knows better than to be impolite at someone else's dinner table.

"It's okay. I actually have two dessert options." Scarlett walks out of the room and returns a minute later with a dish in each hand. "We have apple pie and cherry cheesecake."

She sets both desserts down in the middle of the table, and I groan. "Cherry cheesecake is my favorite."

"I know." She smiles. "That's why I made it. And apple pie is Dad's favorite, although I didn't make it. Sorry, Daddy, yours is from Scooter's."

"I don't care where it came from, Scarlett girl, so long as I know where it's goin'."

"Where's it goin'?" Chloe asks.

Rick pats his stomach. "Right in here."

Scarlett rolls her eyes. "He's totally not joking. What's your favorite dessert, Chloe?"

"Double fudge brownies."

"Ooh. Good choice. Next time, I'll make some."

"Really?"

"Heck, yeah. Who doesn't love double fudge brownies? But since I don't have them tonight, which would you like to have?"

Chloe contemplates for all of two seconds and blurts, "Cheesecake."

"More pie for me," Rick says, sliding the apple pie across the table. He grabs his fork and goes to dig in.

"Dad!"

"What?"

"Aren't you going to share?"

"Would you like a slice, sweetheart?"

"No, but we have guests."

"Chloe already asked for cheesecake, and you know what Tucker is havin', which means...I get the pie."

37

Scarlett just shakes her head when her dad scoops out a bite and shovels it into his mouth.

We're all laughing and talking when the front door opens. Alexis walks in with two Tupperware containers and stops when she sees us sitting around the table. Her smile falters as her eyes sweep past Scarlett, and while I understand where the animosity comes from, it pisses me off. Scarlett deserves some credit for trying, and Alexis seems unwilling to give it to her.

"What did you guys have for dinner?"

"Grilled chicken, loaded baked potatoes, and asparagus," Chloe says, looking proud since she helped Scarlett cook.

"Tucker, you didn't have to cook for them," she chides.

"I didn't. Scarlett did."

Alexis laughs and then sobers when she realizes she's the only one. "Wait. You're serious?"

"As a stroke." We all look at Rick, and he shrugs. "Too soon?"

"Way too soon. And you are talking about my sister, Scarlett, right?"

"Why do you find that so hard to believe?" Scarlett asks.

"Because you don't cook."

Scarlett pushes away from the table and stands up. "How do you know? You don't even know me."

"I know you well enough. You don't cook. You don't clean. You don't come home. In fact, I don't know what you can do other than prance around and look pretty."

The defeated look Scarlett wore earlier is right back on her beautiful face, and I could kill Alexis for putting it there. We all sit stunned, watching the sisters stare each other down. Twelve years ago, it would've ended in a screaming match, but Scarlett seems to have lost that fire inside of her.

Or maybe she's just matured more than any of us have given her credit for.

The thought rolls through my head at the same time Scarlett grabs her plate and disappears into the kitchen. I hear her put it in the sink. A few seconds later, the back door opens and closes.

6

~SCARLETT~

I CAN'T STAND it for another second.

I set my plate in the sink and hurry outside where the heat is still oppressive. It's so humid, it's like breathing in mist.

But it's always been quiet out here, and at least I don't have Lexi's hateful eyes staring back at me.

"Go apologize," I hear Dad say. His voice is hard, and it pisses me off that Lexi's getting him riled up. The man just had a stroke, for God's sake!

"Absolutely not," she replies.

"I'm disappointed in you, Lexi. She's your sister. She cooked a delicious meal, and you just made her feel like shit."

"I can't believe this. She's back for a few days, and you're already on her side."

I roll my eyes and sit on the picnic table. I may be the celebrity, but Lexi's always been the dramatic one in the family.

"There aren't sides," Dad yells. "We're a family."

"Family doesn't leave and never come back," Lexi counters. "Your little girl went twelve years without so much as setting foot in her hometown. She didn't even come when I graduated high school."

"She was on tour," Dad says.

In Japan, as a matter of fact. I hated that I missed her graduation, and I tried to reschedule the tour, but it was set in stone before the school chose a graduation date that year.

"Or my college graduation," Lexi continues. I really should have put A/C in Dad's house last year so we could keep the house closed up and I wouldn't have to hear this.

"She had an award show," Dad replies.

I won a Grammy for *Small Town Girl* that night. I called Lexi to congratulate her on her graduation. She refused to speak to me and didn't even thank me for the car I gave her as a gift.

"What about when Lucy and Declan were born?"

My heart stalls.

"She tried," Dad reminds her. "You told her not to."

I wanted to be here *so badly*. I called Lexi at least once a week for both kids and told her to be sure to give me a heads-up when she went into labor because I wanted to hold her babies more than anything.

Instead, she told me that it wasn't a big deal and that I'd see them later. She wanted the births to be *quiet* and intimate.

And she made it clear that that didn't include me.

So, I sent all of the items on her registry and paid for a year's worth of housekeeping.

"And what about Lucy's first birthday?" she asks, referring to her oldest daughter.

Dad doesn't respond to that one. The truth is, by that time, it was clear to me that I wasn't needed or wanted here, so I stopped making an effort. It was easy to get swept up in my life in Nashville and let Lexi live her life here in New Hope.

"She must really love her family, huh, Dad?"

I can hear the sarcasm and the hurt in my sister's voice, and then the door slams shut. I hang my head in my hands and sigh.

Up until Dad's stroke, I never felt guilty about my decision to move to Nashville. It was the best thing I ever did. My career is the absolute best part of my life.

But since I've been home, the guilt has set in like a lead weight in my stomach, and I cried myself to sleep last night.

Not coming home didn't mean that I didn't love my family or that I didn't think about them. Because I did. I made sure that Lexi and her family had everything they could ever want and need.

And I've taken care of my dad. This house is state-of-the-art. I supplement his retirement income so he never has to worry. And he comes to stay with me in Nashville several times a year.

I love my family, and I take care of them.

But I should have come home more.

I can admit that to myself now.

I take a deep breath and stare up at the bright moon that's just moved out from behind a stray cloud. The stars glow. Crickets chirp, and I can see lightning bugs whizzing about in Tucker's yard.

It's as familiar as my own face, even after all this time.

But it's still not home.

"Do you think this thing will hold the two of us?" Tucker asks. I'm not startled, I heard him come through the back door. I don't say anything but slide to my right, giving him space to sit next to me.

"You okay?" he asks.

I shrug, but I still don't say anything. I'm afraid that once I start talking, I won't stop because Tucker's always been one of the few people that I can pour my guts out to, and he's not that person anymore.

God, I miss him.

He leans back, watching the night sky. I can feel the heat coming off him. He's not a boy anymore. No, Tucker grew into a strong, handsome man with muscles for days. His smile is kind, with just a hint of mischief. He smells like soap, and he makes me yearn for things I never knew I wanted.

I still don't know that I want them, not really.

But I need to talk about this, and Tucker deserves an apology.

"I always felt lost," I say, breaking the silence. "Like I was walking around in a fog, trying to find my way—attempting to find that special place where I belonged. I never found it. When I got to Nashville, everything just sort of clicked into place for me. I can't explain it, but for the first time, I felt at home. I should've come back to New Hope. But, honestly, I didn't think anyone would care if I stayed away."

"Scarlett—"

"Just let me get this out, okay? I need to get it out." Tucker nods, and I continue. "My relationship with Lexi was rocky at best, and it didn't take long after the move to find out that my friends weren't really my friends. They were acquaintances. And let's not forget how being in a small town means that people talk like you're not standing right there, listening to every word. I knew what they all said about my mama, and how her actions made them feel about me. I'm not stupid. Lexi was too little to hear it, or maybe she just didn't care. But I did.

"And then there was you…"

"Me?" he asks, surprised.

"You probably won't believe this, but I thought about you every single day. I can't tell you how many times I picked up the phone to tell you about whatever cool thing happened that day, or just because I wanted to hear your voice." I feel the tears welling up again, but I swallow hard, determined not to cry in front of this man twice in one day.

"Why didn't you?" he asks softly and reaches over to take my hand in his. With just that little touch, it's as if the whole world is set to rights.

"Because I didn't deserve you. I didn't deserve your friend-ship. God, Tucker, I was a bitch to you in school, and I can't tell you how sorry I am for that. I wish I had a good reason for it, but I don't. I was just mean and lost and…you know that saying that we hurt the ones we love the most?"

He nods, not looking me in the eyes. I want to hug him close and beg him to forgive me. I settle for squeezing his hand.

"You were my best friend. I didn't treat you like that in public, but it's the truth. You were my *only* friend. And I hated that. I hated that no one else saw the Scarlett you did. And rather than fix it—fix myself—I took it out on you. God, Tucker, can you ever forgive me?"

"Only if you can forgive me."

All of the breath rushes from my lungs. "For what?"

"For the way I talked to you last night when I brought over the spaghetti."

"I deserved it."

"No, you didn't. I was rude and disrespectful. I'm not gonna lie, Scarlett, you hurt me when you left. You were my best friend, and then you were just…gone. I hate to admit that I lost myself after you left. So, I guess the saying is true because when you did finally come back, instead of giving you a hug and telling you how much I missed you, I got angry."

"You had every right to get angry," I insist, wanting so badly to ask him why he thinks he lost himself. But we're not there yet, and I don't have the right to ask those questions.

"I don't want to be angry, and I sure as hell don't want to fight with you, Scarlett."

"I don't want that either," I reply and lean my cheek on his shoulder. The warmth of his body radiates through me, and I find myself melting against him.

"Does that mean you forgive me for being a complete dick?"

I grin and glance up at him. "I forgive you. Now, what about you?"

"What about me?" he asks, and I roll my eyes and push away from him. Despite the heat, my hand feels cold after he lets me go.

He reaches over with a smile and brushes my hair behind my ear, and I can't help but lean into his touch as his finger slides along my cheek.

It never felt like this when Tucker touched me when we were kids—full of electricity and awareness. It's scary and exciting all at once.

He lowers his face until he's just inches from my lips. I swear to Jesus, the man is going to kiss me, but instead, he says, "I forgive you, Scarlett Jane."

My eyes fall to his full lips. He's breathing a little faster than normal. My body is tight with anticipation and a new longing that I don't recognize but want to explore.

"No one's called me that since I was seventeen."

"Good."

"Hey, Dad! You have to see this," Chloe yells, busting through the back door. "I'm teaching Rick to play gin rummy, and he's totally beating me. It's like he's gifted or something!"

Tucker holds my gaze, humor filling his whiskey-colored eyes.

He pulls back and glances over at Chloe.

"He's not gifted," I reply and stand. "He taught *me* to play that game."

"You're a shark!" Chloe yells as she hurries back inside, making both me and Tucker laugh.

"She's so great, Tuck," I say softly.

"She's the best," he agrees.

"Where's her mom?" The words fly from my mouth before I have a chance to think them over.

His eyes whip to mine in confusion. "You don't know?"

"How would I? I haven't been here for a while, remember?"

He shakes his head, and I have the distinct feeling that I just said something *very* wrong.

"You know," he says as he stands from the table. "I've come to grips with the fact that you didn't come home all those years. But now you're saying you never even *asked* about me? I never came up in conversation with your dad?"

"Of course, you did, Tuck. But it's not like my dad is going to tell me all about your marriage, even if he knew the details. My dad's not a gossip."

"Because there wasn't a marriage to talk about." Tucker walks away from me to the end of the back porch and shoves his hands into the pockets of his cargo shorts, staring at the lightning bugs.

"You don't have to talk about it," I offer, but he shakes his head and turns back to me.

"I'm sorry for overreacting."

"Maybe it's habit?" I offer, earning a half-smile.

"One I need to break," he agrees. "Frankly, I think tonight has been good, and I'd rather not taint it with my shady past."

"Oh, it's shady? Now I really need to know. Let's pop some popcorn, and you can give me all the scandalous details."

"Still a smartass, I see."

"That's never going to change, Tucker Lee."

His lips twitch. "Clearly, we've made up if we're using our full names."

"Or we're mad at each other. My dad used to call me Scarlett Jane when I was in trouble."

"I'm not mad," Tucker says with a slow shake of his head.

"Me either," I breathe. "But, Tuck?"

"Yeah."

"I want to know everything. From the minute I left."

"How long are you going to be here?"

"For as long as it takes."

He tilts his head to the side, watching me. It's implied that I'm here for as long as it takes for my father to heal, but now it means so much more than I ever expected.

"Good answer."

7

~ TUCKER ~

"I'll take a beer." Scooter plops onto a lounge chair and nods toward the cooler at my feet.

"I bet you will," I say, flipping the burgers. "I'm a little busy here. Get it yourself."

"You're standing right there."

Dean rolls his eyes, grabs Scooter a beer, and tosses it to him.

"Thank you, Dean." Scooter pops the top and leans back. "You've always been my favorite cousin."

"Fuck off."

"Language." Mom smacks me on the back of the head and peers over my shoulder at the food on the grill. "How are those burgers coming, sweetheart?"

"You can't hit me on the back of the head and then call me *sweetheart*."

"I'm your mother, I can do whatever I want, and you know better than to cuss with Chloe around."

"She's in the house. It's not like she heard me."

"You tell him, Aunt Theresa." Scooter salutes my mom with his beer, and she ruffles his hair.

"You're such a good boy, Scooter."

Dean laughs, spewing beer across the deck. "Scooter, good? You have met him before, right?"

"See what I put up with?" Scooter sticks his lower lip out in a pout, and of course, Mom falls for it—hook, line, and sinker.

She pats Scooter's cheek and smiles fondly at her only nephew before coming back over to me. "How much longer on those?"

"Ten minutes, tops."

"Don't forget to make mine well-done. You know how I feel about pink in the center."

"I know, Ma. You remind me that every time I grill."

She stares at me for a few seconds and then furrows her brow. "Are you okay, honey? You seem kind of crabby today."

"I'm fine."

"You know"—Scooter kicks his legs over the side of his chair and sits up—"I thought he seemed a little fussy today, too."

Fussy? What am I, two? I roll my eyes and concentrate on the food. "I'm fine. Just tired, that's all."

Because I was up all night thinking about Scarlett and the hooded look to her eyes right before Chloe walked outside.

"Your lack of sleep wouldn't have anything to do with a certain someone who's back in town, would it?" Dean asks.

I love my brother, but I'm going to kill him for saying that in front of Mom.

"What certain someone?" Mom swoops in like flies on shit. "Who's back in town?"

"No one, Ma."

"Scarlett Kincaid." Scooter shrugs when I look at him. "What? She was going to find out sooner or later."

Mom's eyes bounce between Scooter and Dean before she turns fully toward me. "Scarlett is home? I'd hardly call her *no one*. How long has she been here? Have you seen her? What did you talk about?"

Scooter hands his beer to Dean and brings a finger to his mouth.

"You knew that Rick had a stroke, right?" I ask.

"Yes, but I didn't expect it to bring Scarlett home," she says, while Scooter mouths *"oh, Scarlett,"* wraps his arms around the pretend country music star and proceeds to make out with her behind my mother's back.

My lips twitch, but I clear my throat and keep my expression even. "He's her dad. Of course, she came home. Give her a little credit." I know Mom isn't Scarlett's biggest fan, and Scarlett might be self-centered, but she's a good person at her core.

"I'm just shocked, that's all. Is she staying with Rick?"

Here we go with the twenty questions.

"Yep."

"Have you talked to her or not?"

"Uh-huh."

"How long is she in town for?"

"No clue. Ask her yourself."

"Are you two...?"

I set the spatula down and lift an eyebrow. "Are we what?"

Scooter whips an imaginary condom from his pocket, tears it open with his teeth and pretends to roll it down his shaft.

"Copulating. Are you two copulating?"

Scooter stops thrusting his hips long enough to frown at the back of Mom's head. *"Copulating?"* he mouths. Dean tries to hold in his laugh but loses the battle. He stands up and shakes his head.

"Oh, come on, Dean," Mom chides. "You're a grown man. You too, Scooter. Wipe the grin from your face."

"Do you have to use the word *copulating*?" Dean asks, curling his lip. "Why can't you just ask him if he's screwing around with Scarlett?"

"Okay." Mom looks at me, her head tilted contemplatively. "Are you and Scarlett—?"

"No." I hold up a hand, stopping her and this conversation from going any further. "We're not copulating, or anyth—"

"What's copulating?" Chloe asks, stepping outside. The screen door slams shut behind her. I've asked her a million times to close the door so it doesn't slam. Clearly, my words have gone in one ear and out the other.

"Christ." I look up at the sky and pray for patience to deal with my family. "Nothing you need to worry about."

"I'm gonna go check on the potatoes and tell your dad and aunt and uncle that the food is almost ready." Mom gives me a *good-luck-with-Chloe* look before slipping through the back door.

"Fine, don't tell me, I'll just look it up later on the iPad," Chloe says, causing Scooter's eyes to widen, and Dean to choke on his beer.

I level her with my best firm-dad look. "Chloe."

She holds up her hands. "I'm kidding. Hey, Uncle Dean. Hi, Scooter," she says, giving Dean a hug.

Dean was a big help when Chloe was little and has always been like a second dad to her. I'm grateful that she's stayed close to him as she's gotten older, and I know he appreciates it, too.

"How's it going, kiddo?" Dean kisses the side of her head.

"Good."

"You're getting so big."

"Dad says I look just like my mom."

My heart stutters inside my chest. I always try to answer Chloe's questions about her mom as best as I can because Valerie is a sore subject with me. She left our little girl without a mother, and that's something I can't get past.

Dean looks at me before dragging his eyes back to Chloe. "Your mom was beautiful," he says, tucking Chloe's hair behind her ear. "Won't be long, and your dad will be fighting the boys away with a stick."

"You don't have a boyfriend, yet, do you?" Scooter asks.

Chloe blushes and shakes her head. "No, but I have my first dance on Friday."

Shit, I forgot about that.

"Wow. Your first dance." Scooter grabs his beer and sits back in the lounge chair. He takes a pull from his bottle and stares off at the sky. "Next thing we know, you'll be off to college and getting married."

"Whoa," I say, shaking my head. "One thing at a time. I'm not ready for her to grow up quite that fast. And speaking of your dance, what're you going to wear?"

"You promised you'd take me shopping. We're running out of time, Dad."

"You have a ton of dresses in your closet. Can't you wear one of them?"

Chloe looks at me like I've grown a second head. "No. I need a new one. And matching shoes. Everyone has *seen* those dresses, Dad. And most of them are for little girls anyway."

"You *are* a little girl," I remind her, only to be given the preteen scowl I've come to know and hate.

"This is why I refuse to ever have a daughter," Scooter announces. "Too high-maintenance."

"Oh, come on, I'm good for all sorts of stuff."

"Like what?"

"Well, I'm perceptive." Chloe taps her finger to her lips, thinking it over.

"Do you even know what that means?" Scooter asks.

"Yes, but the real question is, do you?"

Dean and I bust up laughing. I love my girl. She's smart as a whip. She gets her good looks from her mom, but every other thing about Chloe is all me.

"Good one." Scooter finishes off his beer and sets it on the ground beside his chair. "But I'm going to need you to back it up. Tell me something about your dad that I can use against him later."

Chloe grins. "Dad likes Scarlett."

"We all like Scarlett. Tell me something I don't know."

"He *likes her*, likes her. He almost kissed her last night."

"*What?*" Scooter flies up in his seat, and Dean's jaw drops.

"Chloe." When did my daughter turn on me? And why was I so careless when she was close by last night? I've always kept other women out of Chloe's life, and I sure as hell haven't brought one home. She's never even seen me hold a woman's hand. "I didn't almost kiss her."

Chloe shrugs. "That's what it looked like to me. You don't have to be embarrassed, Dad. I like her. If you want to kiss her, you can. I approve."

Scooter pats the chair next to him. "Tell me everything."

"Well, when I ran outside, Dad was holding Scarlett's cheek, and their faces were really close together. Like, super close. He was totally gonna kiss her."

"Chloe, go inside and tell your grandma and Aunt Laura that I'm pulling the burgers off the grill."

"Fine." She huffs but knows better than to argue with me.

"Chloe, be a dear and grab me another beer before you go back inside."

I kick Scooter's chair. "Get it yourself. My daughter isn't your maid."

"It's okay." Chloe grabs a beer from the cooler and hands it to Scooter.

"Thanks for the info. And the beer," he says, taking it from her. "You're my favorite second cousin."

"Actually, I'm your first cousin, once removed."

"Huh?" Scooter shields his eyes from the sun and frowns up at her.

"Never mind." Chloe disappears inside.

"Tucker?"

I ignore Scooter and flip the burgers one last time. "I'm not talking about her with you."

"Fine. You listen. I'll talk." He stands up and walks to me. "You've had a crush on that girl since the third grade, and then she fled this town faster than a nun from a whore house, your feelings be damned. She's a superstar, Tuck. Famous beyond any of our imaginations."

"I get that."

"I don't think you do. She can do anything, go anywhere, have anyone."

"Are you trying to tell me I'm not good enough?"

"Hell, no." Scooter shakes his head. "If anything, you're too good for her."

I wouldn't go that far.

"Look, all I'm saying is watch out for that one. Your life is here, and well…hers isn't."

"I know that."

"Good." With a final nod of his head, Scooter walks inside, leaving me alone with Dean, who watches me carefully.

"You gonna warn me against her, too?"

"Nope." Dean shakes his head. "It wouldn't do any good. You've never cared what other people think. I learned a long time ago that you always do what you want to do."

"But…" Because there's always a *but.*

"*But,* I think you should tread lightly. She broke your heart once. I don't put it past her to do it again."

"She didn't break my heart." I was eighteen and in lust. I had no clue what love was at the time. And now, well, now I'm older and wiser and know better than to fall victim to whims evoked by a pretty girl.

"Whatever you have to tell yourself." Dean claps a hand on my shoulder. "Just take it slow and don't get too attached."

When the back door shuts, my eyes drift to Rick's house. Scarlett is standing in her dad's kitchen near the sink. She glances up and catches me looking at her through the window.

Dean's words echo in my head, and all I can think is: *easier said than done. I've never had any sense when it comes to this girl.*

She lifts a hand and waves, her smile slow and soft.

I am so screwed.

"Absolutely not."

"What's wrong with this one?" Chloe lifts her arms and looks at herself in the mirror. "It's cute."

"It's too short."

"You said that about the last three dresses."

"Chloe, I'm not buying you a dress that short, end of story. Maybe you should try on a long one."

"I don't want to try on a long dress. Long dresses aren't in this season. All of my friends are wearing short dresses."

"If all of your friends jumped off a cliff, would you follow?"

Chloe rolls her eyes and stomps into the dressing room. I smile to myself and lean back in the chair to wait for Chloe.

"This one is it, Dad."

Thank God, because I don't know how much more of this I can take, and we've only been here for—I look at my watch—thirty minutes.

Chloe squeals and sashays out of the dressing room in a red, strapless dress. If she bends over, she'll flash the entire world. "Where's the other half?"

"Other half?"

"Of the dress. Chloe, this one is shorter than the last. And it's strapless. No way. Try on the next one."

"There isn't a next one, Dad. This is *the* dress."

"This is a dress, but it's not *the* dress because I'm not paying for that scrap of material."

"Ugh." Chloe whirls around and growls. "Why are you being so difficult?"

"I could ask you the same thing," I mumble.

"Daughters," a woman says, dropping down beside me on the couch. "Can't live with 'em, can't live without 'em."

"Oh, I bet I could live without her," I joke.

The woman smiles and then laughs when she says, "I could probably live without mine, too. I'm Laura." She holds out her hand, and I shake it.

"Tucker. That lovely girl that just rolled her eyes at me is my daughter, Chloe."

"She's beautiful."

"Thank you. Which one of these prepubescent tween princesses belongs to you?"

Laura points to a set of twin girls fawning over the jewelry rack.

"Oh my God, you have two? How does that even work?"

"Well," she says, crossing her legs, "it's double the hair in my sink, double the mess, double the food, double the laundry, double the eye rolls and growls and tears."

I shudder. "You deserve some sort of medal. The hair I could handle, the tears I could not."

Chloe sulks out from behind a curtain, and Laura and I both look up.

"Yes!" I jump up and turn Chloe so she can look at herself in the mirror. "This one is my favorite."

"It's hideous."

"No, it's not." The skirt is three-quarter-length, cutting off mid-calf, the straps are nice and thick with a high chest line, and there are rhinestones. Every girl loves rhinestones. "You said you didn't have any more dresses to try on."

"Because this dress is awful. I don't even know how it ended up in my pile."

"I put it there."

Chloe looks at me blandly. "I'm not wearing this dress out in public."

"Oh, come on, you're being dramatic." I turn to Laura. "Would you tell her that she looks wonderful?"

"I look like I'm eighty."

Laura pinches her lips together and tilts her head. "Well…"

"See." Chloe spins around and disappears before I have a chance to argue.

Dress shopping is officially a form of parental torture. God help me when prom rolls around. If I can't survive a junior high dance, there's no way I'll make it through prom.

The door rips open, and Chloe shoves past me, the stack of dresses in her arms.

"We'll keep looking," I say, following her through the store.

"What's the point? You're just going to hate every single one I pick out."

"That isn't true."

Chloe whirls around. "Yes, it is. Everything is too short or cut too low in the back, or the straps are too thin."

"You're eleven years old, Chloe. I'm not going to let you walk out of the house looking like you're twenty."

She opens her mouth to argue, but I've had enough.

"Yell at me one more time, and you're grounded. I am not arguing with you about this in the middle of the store. Now, you can either stop throwing a tantrum and we can keep looking for dresses, or we're going home."

"Fine, let's go home." Chloe finds a sales associate, hands off the dresses, and heads straight for the door. "You didn't even want to come to begin with."

"That's not true."

"Whatever."

God, I hate that word.

The ride home is silent. Not in the comfortable sense, but in the *I'm so pissed off at you I can't even breathe* sense from my eleven-year-old.

If this is how it is when she's prepubescent, I don't even want to *think* about how she'll be in five years.

Lord, have mercy.

I pull into my driveway, and before I've even cut off the engine, Chloe hurries out of the car, slamming the door behind her way harder than necessary and then stomps up onto the front porch.

"Come back here," I say after climbing out of the vehicle.

"I want to go to my room."

"I've had it with your mouth today, young lady. I said, come back here."

"You're being ridiculous," she says when she turns around, but when she sees the stern look on my face, she looks down and finishes the sentence with, "sir."

"You owe me an apology for yelling at me in public like that."

She frowns. "I'm sorry if I was disrespectful. I'm just so *frustrated.*"

"Yeah, well, join the club."

Chloe's head comes up, and her face turns from a frown to a tentative smile.

"Hi, Scarlett."

"Hi, you two," Scarlett says as she walks across her dad's lawn. "I just saw you pull in and thought I'd see what you're up to."

"Dad's yelling at me because I'm a brat," Chloe says, and I rub my hand over the back of my neck in frustration.

"Really?" Scarlett asks.

"No, not really," I reply before Chloe can. "We're having a discussion about dresses for her dance."

"He's incorrigible."

"Dads usually are," Scarlett says with a sigh. "Did you get a dress?"

"No, because he hates everything I like." Chloe sits on the top step of the porch and props her chin in her hand as if all is lost in her world. "I guess I just won't go to the dance since I don't have anything to wear."

"You have a whole closet full of clothes," I remind her, but she just rolls her eyes.

"I have an idea," Scarlett says. "Why don't I take Chloe shopping for a suitable dress?"

"Really?" Chloe's head whips up, her face lighting up with excitement. "You'd take me? That would be so dope."

"You don't have to do that," I say, earning another scowl from my daughter. "I don't want you to feel obligated."

"Sugar, there are few things in this world I feel obligated to do."

Somehow, I don't think that's entirely true.

"I would *love* to get out of the house for a few hours and take this sweet girl shopping. If you don't mind hanging out with my daddy."

"Done." I jump at the chance to spend time with Rick rather than a pouty preteen. And I don't even feel guilty about it. "But there are rules."

"Of course, there are." Scarlett crosses her arms over her chest and cocks a hip to the side. I almost forget what we're talking about. "What are they?"

"What are what?"

Scarlett's lips twitch with humor. "The rules."

"Oh, right. Sorry. One, it needs to hit below the knee. Two, no cleavage. And three, it can't be strapless."

"Basically, I should just wear a nun costume," Chloe says.

"Nah, we can totally work with those rules," Scarlett says. "Let me go grab my handbag, and we'll be on our way."

She hurries back to Rick's house, and Chloe rushes inside ours.

"I'm going shopping with Scarlett Kincaid!"

I wanted to say no. That I have it covered. But the truth is, I *don't* have it covered, and I'm relieved that Scarlett offered to take my daughter shopping.

I'll happily go have my ass handed to me in gin rummy by Rick.

8

~SCARLETT~

Shopping in New Hope isn't easy. In a town this small, the best we can do is a JC Penney or Target. The alternative is to drive up to Charleston, and thanks to Tucker leaving this for the last minute, we don't have time for that.

So, we start at JC Penney.

"This is the one I told Dad I want," Chloe says, making a beeline for a little red dress. She holds it up against her small frame, and at a glance, I'd say it's all the things Tucker said he doesn't want.

Of course.

"Chloe, there are rules, remember?"

"Just let me try it on," she pleads. "I'll show you, it's not that bad."

"Okay. Let's grab a few for you, sound good?"

"I want this one," she whispers, but I pretend not to hear her. Chloe's as strong-willed as her father. It's no wonder they butt heads from time to time.

Reminds me of me with my dad. I'll have to apologize to him later for being difficult.

"I don't wear pink," Chloe says when I hold up a blush-colored dress. "Ever."

"This one's out then."

She nods, and I reach for a cute little black dress.

"I don't like black."

"Chloe, why do I get the feeling the only color you like is red?"

She grins and shrugs one shoulder. "Red is my favorite."

"Okay, I get it. You want *that* dress. But you have to work with me here. It's called compromise. If you're not willing to budge, no one gets what they want, and everyone is just angry. And that's no fun."

"I bet you don't have to compromise."

"Why do you say that?"

"Because you're rich and famous and can have anything you want."

"Think again, kiddo." I grab the black dress, making Chloe scowl, but I ignore her. "I have to compromise all the time. Because I'm a grown-up. So, if you want to be taken seriously, you need to shed some of the attitude and be more open-minded. I think you hurt your dad's feelings today."

Chloe frowns, the first chink in her carefully erected armor. "I didn't mean to hurt his feelings."

"I know. It's tough when you think you know what's best, and your dad's idea of that is different from yours. I was raised by a single dad, too."

"Oh, yeah. It's not so bad. My dad's really great. He's a good person, and I usually get pretty much what I want. But, sometimes, he just doesn't understand being a *girl*. You know?"

"Of course. Because he's a boy, so it's hard for him to understand." I lead her to the dressing rooms and hang the dresses on the rack inside, then step out while Chloe changes. "Start with the black one. We'll look at the red one last."

She sighs heavily, and I smile.

"Why doesn't your mom take you shopping?" I ask and bite my lip, hoping I didn't cross a line with the question. But the truth is, I'm *dying* to know more about her mother.

"I never met her," she says matter-of-factly. "It's just been Dad and me since I was born. He says I look a lot like her, but he doesn't tell me too much else. I think it makes him sad."

"Did she die?" I ask.

"No, she didn't want me."

There's no sadness in her voice. No regret. Just facts, and that breaks my heart because I know what it's like to have your mom not want you.

How could *anyone* not want this wonderful little girl? I mean, I'm the least maternal person I know, and I would scoop her up in a heartbeat.

Chloe comes out of the dressing room wearing the black dress I chose.

"And don't feel sorry for me because my dad is awesome, and we don't need her."

"I couldn't agree with you more. You and your dad are doing great."

She walks to the mirror and frowns. "This one isn't bad, but I don't love it."

"Hmm." I tug on the hemline. It hits her at mid-calf, but it makes her legs look stubby. And I don't like where it sits on her hips. "This one is a no."

"Told you."

She walks back into the dressing room to change.

"Anyway," she continues, "the only thing I know about my mom is that her name is Valerie, and she grew up here, but her family doesn't live here anymore."

My mind whirls, trying to think who this Valerie could be.

"So, you don't even see her parents?"

"Nope. I have Nana and Papa, and Rick. He's like a grandpa to me."

"Of course."

Valerie? Who the heck is —?

Holy shit. Could her mom be—? No. It's not possible. Hell would freeze over before Tucker would touch *her*.

Just the thought of it makes me want to gag.

No way.

Before I can ponder it further, Chloe marches out of the dressing room, her chin raised a bit defiantly, sporting the strapless red dress.

"I like *this* one."

She walks to the mirror and smiles at her reflection. I have to admit, it's cute, the girl has good taste.

Yes, the skirt hits above the knee, but only by about an inch. It's not form-fitting, and it's much more flattering than the black dress. However, I agree with Tucker that the top is too revealing.

"So, here's the thing with this dress, Chloe. It's super cute." She smiles triumphantly. "But it needs something more on top."

"You sound like my dad."

"He's not wrong." She shakes her head, but I take her shoulders in my hands and hold her gaze in the mirror. "Think about it like this. You're a beautiful girl. There will be so much time to grow into dresses that show a bit more skin, but you don't want to show everyone all the goods first thing out of the gate. You need to be a mystery."

"A mystery?"

"Oh, yeah. Be mysterious. Wear pretty clothes, don't let them wear you. That means *you're* the gorgeous one, not the dress."

She tilts her head to the side, thinking it over. "Yeah. I like that."

"So, we're going to add a little black shrug, maybe a shimmery necklace. It's all about accessories."

"See, Dad wouldn't have thought of this."

"Well, that's what you have me for, isn't it?"

I wink, and with a feeling of victory, Chloe and I go find the rest of her outfit.

———

"SEE, DAD?" Chloe says as she walks out of her bedroom, ready to give us a fashion show. We're sitting on the couch, and I'm watching Tucker's face.

"Isn't that the dress I shot down?" He glances at me, and I smile brightly.

"You're right, it is. But hear us out." I hurry next to Chloe. "The dress barely skims her knees. And trust me, we tried other dresses that hit her below the knee, and they chop her off awkwardly."

"But they *cover* the knees."

I fight the impulse to roll my eyes.

"Please, hear me out." He nods once. "This black cardigan serves two purposes. One, it dresses it down a bit and makes it more age-appropriate, *and* it covers her arms and shoulders. We added the thin black belt and a sparkly necklace, and with her hair curled, she'll look absolutely stunning."

"I swear I won't take the sweater off, Dad. I promise."

His gaze shifts between the two of us, and I bite my lip, waiting for the verdict. Finally, he sighs.

"Okay, it looks nice. But you have to keep that sweater on."

"Oh my God, I totally promise," Chloe says, bouncing to Tucker and throwing her arms around his neck. "Thank you, Daddy."

"You're welcome. Go hang your dress up so it doesn't wrinkle."

"Can I watch YouTube for a while?"

"One hour," he says before kissing her cheek and watching her skip happily up the stairs to her bedroom.

"Thank you," I say softly.

"No, thank *you*. I wouldn't have thought of the sweater, and she would have been mad at me for weeks."

"It was fun, actually."

He stares at me in surprise, making me giggle.

"I know this is a shocker, but shopping is fun for girls. Next time, I'll take her to Charleston so we can shop properly."

He tilts his head to the side. "Do you think you'll still be here for a next time?"

The words just flew out of my mouth without thinking. But the truth is, I don't know how long I'll be in town.

"I don't know," I admit.

He nods, and I sit next to him on the couch, the silence awkward.

"How's my dad?" I ask.

"He's good. Lexi came over for lunch, so I came home. She's over there now."

"I saw her car when I pulled in." I steel myself for my next question. "Tuck, is Valerie Brown Chloe's mom?"

He blinks, taken aback by the question, and then his face transforms to the one I know so well. The one that says: *guilty.*

"No." I stand and shake my head. "Tell me it's not true."

"I can't tell you that."

"Tucker, I *hated* her. She was so mean!"

"Yeah, well…"

"How could you even touch her? Ew." I shiver. "I don't even want to think about it."

"Then stop thinking about it."

"Tucker." I groan and cover my face. "*Valerie Brown*?"

"Maybe I knew you hated her. And you left."

"Hold up. Are you telling me you boned Vicious Valerie because I hurt your feelings?"

"Well, when you put it like that, it sounds childish, but"—he shrugs a shoulder, and I stare at him in disbelief—"she did give me Chloe."

"And Chloe is wonderful, but Valerie Brown?" I whisper, then shiver again. "We can't speak of this ever again. It's not okay."

"You're so dramatic."

"I can't believe you gave it to the mean girl."

"Stop saying it like that," he says, laughing.

"It's true. Yuck. Okay, I have to go home and scrub my mind's eye with a hot poker."

"Okay, drama girl. Thanks for being nice to my kid."

"Yeah, well, I like her. A lot more than I like you right now."

"I can live with that," he replies and follows me to the door. He opens it for me, and as I walk past him, he pulls me against him into a strong hug, his arms folding around me firmly. I wrap my arms around his middle and breathe in soap and sunshine.

He smells the same as he did all those years ago.

"I missed you," he whispers against my hair before pressing a kiss to the top of my head.

Tears spring to my eyes, and before I make a fool of myself, I nod and pull away.

"I missed you more."

And with that, I hurry across the yard to my dad's house, feeling Tucker's eyes pinned to my back the entire way.

IT'S BEEN ALMOST a week since I took Chloe shopping. Her dance should be tonight, and I'd love to go help her get ready, but I haven't been invited, and I'm hanging out with Dad tonight.

I've spent the last five days shuffling him to and from therapy, watching way more reality TV than I thought possible, and enjoying spending time with him while trying to get glimpses of our ridiculously handsome neighbor.

Chloe came over to see us after school until Tucker got home from work. It seems that's her usual routine and has been since her first day of kindergarten. I kind of love that my father has had such a strong role in Chloe's life, and sad that I didn't know her at all until now.

I never would have imagined that I'd miss out on so much here in New Hope. Which I know makes me sound like a self-centered bitch.

"Hi there, Lexi," Dad says when my sister walks through the front door. She's carrying a bag of groceries in one hand and a baking pan in the other.

"Hello," she says, smiling at Dad. When her eyes turn to me, the smile doesn't fall from her face, which shocks the hell out of me. "I thought I'd come over and hang out for a while."

"Well, this is a nice surprise," Dad replies.

"I brought chicken cordon bleu with me," she continues, marching into the kitchen. "Scarlett, will you please come in here?"

So you can yell at me again? No, thank you.

I don't move, and Dad gives me *the look.*

"Sure." I walk into the kitchen and stop short when Lexi smiles at me. It's not a fake smile, either. It's a real one. She must be drunk. "What's up?"

"Look, I know you've been putting in a lot of hours around here. You've done a good job with Dad this week."

I narrow my eyes, wondering when the other shoe will drop.

"Why don't I spend the evening with Dad, and you go take some time for yourself?"

"I'm sorry, I don't mean to sound ungrateful, but am I talking with Alexis Jean Kincaid? My little sister?"

She shrugs. "I'm in a good mood."

"I like it." Without overthinking it, I rush over and give her a hard, fast hug, startling both of us. "Thank you. I'll be home by midnight."

"Have fun," she calls as I walk into the living room with Dad.

"Do you mind if I go out for the evening while you and Lexi hang out?"

"Not at all. Go spend some time with Tucker. Make him take you somewhere nice."

I laugh and shake my head. "I had no idea you were such a romantic, Dad."

I hurry up to my bedroom and change into a pair of jeans with a black button-down top, slip into my cowboy boots, and run a brush through my dark hair. With a few swipes of a makeup brush, I'm ready to go.

I wave to Lexi and Dad, then set off across the yard to Tucker's house.

And just as I approach the front door, I hear yelling inside.

"Just a little makeup!" Chloe yells.

"I said *no* makeup," Tucker replies. "It's bad enough I'm letting you wear that dress. Don't push me on this, Chloe."

I open the door without knocking and smile when both heads turn my way.

"Hi."

"I'm not going," Chloe says, stomping her foot.

Tucker sighs, and before he says anything, Chloe runs upstairs to her bedroom.

"So, this is going well," Tucker says and rubs his hand over his mouth before climbing the stairs after his daughter. I follow behind and listen outside the door.

"Chloe."

"You just want me to look like a baby."

"No, I want you to look like an eleven-year-old."

"It's just a little makeup."

"Um, guys?"

Tucker sighs and looks back at me. His eyes are defeated, and maybe a little sad.

"Can I please help?"

"He won't listen," Chloe says and throws herself over her bed dramatically. Tucker's jaw clenches in frustration.

I don't want to cross a line, but I do want to help.

"Chloe, you need to apologize to your father."

Both heads whip around in surprise.

"What?" Chloe asks.

"You heard me. Remember last week when we talked about compromise and your attitude?"

She cringes and then nods. "Sorry, Dad."

"Now. There is a compromise here. Tucker, if you trust me, I'd be happy to help Chloe with her hair and makeup."

"What about your dad?"

"Lexi is with him. She offered to spend the evening with him so I could have a night off."

"Lexi? As in your sister, Alexis?"

"Shocking, I know. So, what do you say? Can I help Chloe?"

He props his hands on his hips and watches me, then sighs and nods. "Okay. Thank you. But not too much."

"You're welcome. And no clown makeup, I promise." I make a cross over my heart. "Now, this is a girls-only zone. You go wait for the big reveal."

I shoo him out of the room and then turn to Chloe. "You'll never get your way with him if you yell and stomp your foot. You sound like a baby."

"But he makes me so mad."

"I think the feeling's mutual." I sigh and reach for her hairbrush. "Now, let's get down to business. If it's okay with you, I'll help you with your hair and makeup."

"Yes, please. I don't know what I'm doing."

"It's a good thing that I do." I wink and get to work, and before long, we're done.

"Wow," she says when I finally let her look in the mirror. Chloe touches her soft curls, blinks her big, beautiful eyes that are highlighted with just a touch of mascara, and smiles. "I look really pretty."

"You sure do," I agree. "Let's go show your daddy."

I follow Chloe downstairs and into the kitchen where Tucker's doing the dishes. When he looks up at his daughter, he smiles brightly.

"Well, look at you."

"What do you think?" Chloe holds out the skirt of her dress and turns in a circle.

"I think you're the most beautiful girl in the world," he says and hugs her to his side, careful not to mess up her hair. "My little girl isn't so little anymore."

"Dad?"

"Yeah?"

"Can you loosen your grip just a little?"

"Sorry." Tucker gives her one last squeeze and takes a step back. "Now, are you ready to go to the dance?"

"Yes. Can I have my phone?"

"Yep." He takes an iPhone out of a cabinet, turns it on, and passes it to her. "It's fully charged. You may call or text me and Jenny only."

"Can I take some pictures?"

"Yes. And text me when you're ready to come home. The dance ends at nine, so if I don't hear from you by then, I'll be there at eight-fifty-five."

"Yes, sir," Chloe says, the obstinate child from just an hour ago long gone and replaced by an excited preteen. "Let's go."

"I'll see you later," I say, but Tucker frowns.

"Why don't you go with us? I'll take you somewhere to eat after we get rid of the munchkin."

"You're gonna miss me," Chloe says as she walks out the door to the car. Tucker grins, waiting for my answer.

"Sure. I'd like that."

Tucker repeats the rules to Chloe again on the way to the school, and once she's hurried out of the car to join her friends, he pulls away and smiles over at me.

"Where would you like to go?"

"Charlie's," I say immediately, my mouth already salivating at the thought of their chocolate shakes. "I haven't been since I've been home."

"Charlie's it is," he replies.

The place hasn't changed. Red booths line the perimeter of the diner, and white tables and chrome chairs with red seats fill the middle. There's a long soda counter with red stools, and two young girls in white aprons bustling behind it.

Elvis plays on the jukebox, and we're shown to a booth on the far side of the restaurant.

"It's just like I remember it."

"Charlie's doesn't change," Tucker agrees. "They did finally recover all the seats because the vinyl was splitting so bad people's asses were getting cut."

"Well, that's pleasant." I set the menu aside, not even needing to look at it.

"Thanks for helping with Chloe."

"You don't have to thank me. I had fun. I reminded her to check her attitude."

He frowns and sits back, looking out at the parking lot.

Oh, crap. This is what I was afraid of. "I'm sorry if I crossed a line. It's really none of my business. You don't need my input."

"No, I'm not mad. I appreciate the help. Chloe respects you."

I nod and smile at the young waitress when she walks up. Her eyes go wide when she sees that it's me in the booth.

"Hello, Miss Scarlett."

"Hello."

"This is Rachel Laramie's daughter, Heather," Tucker says.

"Oh, hi," I say with a bright smile. "How is your mama?"

"She's good. She's working, as always." Heather pulls out her pen and pad to take our order.

"Well, please tell her I said hi."

"I will. We listen to your music all the time. What can I get you?"

"Bacon cheeseburger with onion rings and a chocolate shake," I say.

"Times two," Tucker adds. Heather writes down the order, nods, and hurries back behind the counter.

"I didn't know Rachel Laramie got married."

"She didn't," Tucker says with a shrug. "She works at the hospital as a nurse."

"Who's Heather's daddy?"

"Rafe McKenna."

I feel my jaw drop. "Rafe McKenna, the science teacher?"

Tucker nods. "I guess they had a thing going all through school. Rachel got pregnant in college, and when word got out, Rafe's wife divorced him."

"Whoa. Rachel is like five years older than us, but how did I not hear about this?"

"Why do you think?"

I shrug. "Yeah, well. I hate town gossip. It's one of the reasons I left. I don't like listening to it, and I don't like spreading it. I was the subject of it for far too long."

"I know."

Our food is delivered quickly, and I dig in, sighing in absolute delight at the familiar sensations on my tongue.

"Smm mmmp."

Tucker laughs. "Say that in English."

"So good." I take a drink of the shake and grin. "Best food in the world. And I've been all over the world, so I know."

"I won't argue."

We eat in silence, both of us hungry. And when our plates are clean, we sit back, regretting our life decisions.

"I ate too much."

"We should have split it," I agree, but Tucker frowns at me.

"Hell, no. I don't share Charlie's food."

"You're so selfish." I toss an onion ring at him, and he pops it into his mouth.

"Yes, ma'am."

Tucker pays the bill, and we walk out to the car, but when he puts the key in the ignition, I stop him.

"Can we talk for a minute?"

"Sure."

"I know I said we'd never speak of it again, but I'm dying to ask some questions."

He sighs. "Okay. Ask."

"Why isn't Valerie around?"

"She didn't want the baby," he says flatly, not looking my way. "She wanted to give her up for adoption. I wanted to keep her. So, my dad drew up papers that she signed, stating I would have sole custody, and she gave up all parental rights."

Tucker's father is a well-respected attorney in New Hope.

"Her parents went along with that?"

"They were ecstatic. We were nineteen, Scar. Val's parents wanted her to wash her hands of it and move on with her life. So, she had Chloe, passed her to me, and never saw her again. Once she recovered, her parents moved them all out to New Mexico or Colorado or something. I haven't heard from her since."

"She just walked away?"

"Yeah." He reaches over to cover my hand with his. "And I know that's a sore subject for you."

"I don't know which is better," I admit. "Valerie leaving before Chloe could know her, or my mom leaving when I was eight."

"Neither way is good," he says.

"Well, I'm going to be really catty and admit that I'm glad she's gone because *I don't like her,* Tuck. She doesn't deserve Chloe."

He laughs and brings my hand to his lips, pressing a kiss to my knuckles.

"I know it makes me a bad person."

I also hate the thought of Tucker having sex with her. It's irrational, but it's there all the same.

I could scratch Valerie's eyes out for ever putting her skanky hands on him.

"What are you thinking?" he says.

"Horrible thoughts."

He raises a brow. "Like?"

"You don't want to know."

"Tell me anyway."

I sigh. "I want to do bodily harm to Vicious Valerie for ever touching you. I'm not good at being jealous, Tucker, but I admit, I am, and I don't like it."

"No?"

"Not even a little."

"Interesting." He leans over, drawing our faces closer together. "I wonder what we could possibly do to make you *not* think about that."

"I don't know," I whisper, watching his full lips as he licks them, imagining what they'd feel like. "What do you think?"

Without answering, he cups my jawline in his big hand and presses his lips to mine. I'd swear the whole universe exploded.

The kiss is soft and sweet. Not tentative. No, he knows what he's doing, and he's damn good at it. But it's gentle, just like Tucker. Thorough. And just as I slide my hand up his firm chest to his face, a rhythmic beep echoes in the car.

"Chloe," he says as he pulls away from me, staring down at me with lust and regret swirling in his eyes.

"You'd better see what she needs."

He pulls his phone out of his pocket. "She's ready to come home."

"It's only eight."

"That's not a good sign."

9

~ TUCKER ~

"CHLOE, WHAT'S WRONG?"

"Nothing. Just drive."

"It's not nothing if you're crying."

She looks up, catching my eye in the rearview mirror. Her cheeks are tear-stained, the makeup she fought so hard for, long gone.

"Did someone hurt you? Did someone touch you?" Kids are cruel these days. My blood boils at the thought of some punk doing something to my baby girl. "What's the twerp's name, I'll—"

"Tuck." Scarlett rests a hand on my arm. "Let's get her home."

Instinctively, I want to fix whatever the problem is now, but maybe Scarlett is right. "Yeah. Okay."

Chloe is silent the entire ride home, and as soon as we pull into the driveway, she darts into the house.

I climb out of the car and, once again, Scarlett stops me.

"Can I offer a piece of advice?"

"Sure, but can you make it quick?"

Scarlett smiles, and I try my hardest not to get sucked into her beautiful web because there's someone else I need to concentrate on.

"I know that you're her daddy and you've spent the last eleven years protecting her and all you want to do is barge in there and demand to know what happened, but don't. Please, don't."

"To hell with that."

"Hear me out." She takes a step forward. "Take it from someone who has been an eleven-year-old girl; the last thing you want to do is make her more upset than she already is. Then she really won't tell you anything. What Chloe needs right now is for you to listen, even if that means understanding that she's not ready to talk about whatever happened."

"I don't know if I can do that."

Scarlett shrugs her shoulder. "You know more about this parenting business than I do. You're her father, and I'm sure you'll make the right decision."

"Where are you going?" I ask when Scarlett turns toward her house.

"Home. I figured you wouldn't want me around for something like this."

I should let her go. Chloe is already getting attached to Scarlett, and this is my opportunity to draw the line in the sand. But I like having Scarlett around just as much as my daughter does—if not more. I've missed Scarlett since the day she left, but I never knew quite how much until she returned.

I don't know what's going to happen between us, but I know that this—whatever *this* is—feels right.

I hold my hand out to her. "Stay."

Scarlett's breath catches. She looks at my hand as though she's not sure if it'll burn her or be the answer to all of life's questions, and then something flashes in her eyes, and she slips her palm into mine.

Her skin is soft and warm, and I give her fingers a gentle squeeze, letting her know how much her staying means to me.

"I've never had to do this," I say as we walk into the house.

"Sure, you have. This can't be the first time Chloe has cried."

"Smartass." I nudge her with my elbow. "This is different than a scraped knee or a broken toy. I always knew this day would come. This is big-girl stuff, and I don't want to screw it up."

"You won't."

Chloe's bedroom door is open. She's face-down on the bed, her head buried in a pillow. I let go of Scarlett's hand and knock softly on the door before I step into the room.

"Can I come in?"

Watching your little girl cry because she's hurt—not physically, but from life—is every dad's worst nightmare. I'm a protector. I'm supposed to shield her from all of the bad things in the world, but I couldn't shield her from this.

Chloe's shoulders jerk as she sobs into the pillow. I sit on the bed beside her and rest a hand on her back. When she was little, I used to cradle her in my lap. We'd snuggle, she'd talk about whatever was bothering her, and then I'd get her a glass of chocolate milk and a snack and all would be right in the world.

If only it were still that easy. With the attitude she's been tossing around lately, I half expect her to pull away, but she doesn't.

"Do you want to talk about what happened?"

"No! Go away."

I can't. How am I supposed to just leave her here? I look up to find Scarlett leaning against the door jam. She tries to smile, but it ends up being more of a frown.

"I love you, Chloe. So much." I bend down and kiss her head. "Whenever you're ready to talk about what happened tonight, I'm here." Her cries grow louder, and the next thing I know, she's in my arms.

Chloe presses her face against my chest, and I hold onto her tighter than I think I ever have. "Oh, sweetheart. Whatever's going on, it's going to be okay, I promise you."

"He laughed at me," she mumbles against my shirt.

"Who?"

She sits up and wipes the tears from her face. "Jimmy."

I hate Jimmy. I'll kill him. "Why did he laugh at you?"

"I don't know." She lifts a shoulder and sucks in a breath. "I asked him to dance, and his friends started laughing, and then some other girls who were standing there started laughing, and then *he* started laughing."

"Did you knee him in the balls?"

"Tucker," Scarlett chides.

Chloe half-laughs, half-cries, and shakes her head. "I ran away and texted you."

"You did the right thing." I pull her back into my arms. "Jimmy's a jerk. Most boys are at that age."

I wish I had some words of wisdom to give to her, but I don't. I don't know what in the hell was going on in that kid's head. Chloe is sweet and smart and beautiful...what's not to love?

"I just don't get it," she says, cuddling against me the way she did when she was a little girl. "When we were at the punch bowl, he told me I looked pretty, but then when I asked him to dance, he acted like a doofus."

"Sounds like he was trying to look cool in front of his friends."

"But he embarrassed me."

"You have nothing to be embarrassed about. You didn't do anything wrong."

"Did something like this ever happen to you?"

I shake my head and push a strand of Chloe's tear-soaked hair behind her ear. "I was never as brave as you."

"What do you mean?"

"It took a lot of courage for you to ask Jimmy to dance. I never built up enough courage to ask the girl I liked to dance." My eyes slide across the room to Scarlett. She straightens her back and watches me.

Chloe follows my gaze. "You wanted to dance with Scarlett, didn't you?"

"Maybe."

Chloe smiles, and the knot in my stomach loosens. "I bet she would've said yes."

Scarlett walks into the room and sits on the other side of the bed by Chloe. "You think too highly of me."

Chloe's brows pinch together. "What do you mean?"

"Well, this isn't easy to admit, especially to someone I admire —that's you by the way," she adds, shoulder-bumping Chloe. "But I wasn't the nicest girl when we were growing up. Actually, I was probably the female version of Jimmy."

"I don't believe it. You're way too nice, and my dad tells me stories about how much fun the two of you had."

I take a breath and listen to Scarlett. "We did have fun together, outside of school. But during school, I wasn't very nice."

"Why?" Chloe asks.

"I wish I had a good answer for you, but I don't. I was insecure and angry at the world. I always worried about what everyone else thought, and I...I just wasn't very nice."

"What changed?" Chloe asks. "You seem to like my dad now."

Scarlett looks at me and grins. "I've always liked your dad. The problem was never him. It was me."

"You think that maybe Jimmy really does like me, but he's too embarrassed to admit it in front of his friends?"

"Maybe. But here's the thing, if he can't admit it in front of his friends, he isn't worth your time. You're young, and lots of boys will come in and out of your life—"

"Not lots," I clarify.

Scarlett rolls her eyes and continues as though I didn't interrupt her. "—but the good ones, the ones that are worth your time, they won't make you cry. The good ones won't laugh at you. They'll make you smile. They'll ask *you* to dance."

"Did my dad used to make you smile?"

"All the time. Still does. Your dad is one of the good ones."

"Do you think that someday a boy will ask me to dance?"

"I know it."

"That's it, I'm going to have to chaperone every dance for the rest of your life."

Chloe giggles. "Please, don't."

I wrap my arm around her shoulders. "I like it so much better when you're laughing."

"I love you, Dad."

"I love you, too. Why don't you take a shower and wash the night away? It'll make you feel better."

"I think you're right. I'm sorry you had to come get me early and that I only wore my dress for a few hours."

"You don't ever have to apologize for calling me to help you. I'm always here for you, Chloe. Today, tomorrow, twenty years from now. I'm always here. You'll get a chance to wear the dress again." I give her one final squeeze and stand up. I hold a hand out for Scarlett. "Come on, I'll walk you home."

"Good night, Chloe," Scarlett says, taking my hand.

"Good night, Scarlett. Thank you for helping me with the dress, and for doing my hair and makeup."

"Anytime. And make sure you hang that dress up," Scarlett says as I tug her out of Chloe's room. "Make sure she hangs that dress up. You should probably have it dry-cleaned, too."

"Dry-clean. Got it."

We step out the front door, and Scarlett rests her head on my shoulder as we walk slowly across the yard.

"You were great in there."

"Really? Because I was totally winging it. I sort of felt like I was flopping around and messing the whole thing up."

Scarlett steps in front of me, grips the front of my shirt, and tugs me forward. "I don't think you *can* mess up. You're a great dad. I wish I could've been around to see you with her when she was younger."

"No, you don't. I was a walking disaster."

"I don't believe that for a second. You're great, Tucker, and not just with Chloe. You're great with the community, and your family, and my dad. It's embedded in your DNA."

"You think I'm great?"

"Mm-hmm."

"I think you're pretty okay," I say, cupping her jaw in my

hands. I brush my thumbs along her cheekbones and tilt her face to mine. "Should we talk about that kiss earlier?"

"I don't think we need to talk about it. I just think we need to do it more often."

"Have I ever told you that I like the way you think?"

"Tucker, shut up and kiss me."

She doesn't have to tell me twice. I lower my mouth to hers.

This feels so surreal.

I've dreamed of being like this with Scarlett for so long. I've dreamed of kissing her and holding her. I've dreamed of what it would be like to feel her body pressed against mine. I never believed it would happen, and now that it has—and still is—I have to convince myself that it's real.

I wrap an arm around her back and deepen the kiss. Her mouth slides over mine with lips that are soft yet confident. She lifts onto her toes. The press of her body against mine is delicious. As she pushes her fingers into my hair, she makes the sexiest sounds—moans and whimpers and murmurs that have my body vibrating with energy—and I want and need to get as close to her as I possibly can.

With one hand on the small of her back, I curl the other around the nape of her neck. I can't get enough of her. My dreams were nothing compared to the reality of having her in my arms. We're a frenzy of hands and tongues, searching and exploring and—

"Oh my God!" Scarlett squeals.

One minute, we're kissing. The next, we're being doused by ice-cold water. Scarlett laughs and holds up her hands. "When did my dad get sprinklers?"

"I installed them last summer," I say, laughing at the situation.

We're both soaked to the bone, but neither of us moves. She's absolutely gorgeous. Her big eyes blink. Water drips from her eyelashes and her nose. The old Scarlett would've been pissed, but the woman in front of me—the woman she is today—looks carefree and happy, and not at all bothered by the wet mop on her head or the makeup running down her face.

"You should probably kiss me again before I have to go inside."

"I thought you'd never ask."

I close the small distance and kiss her. This time, our lips move in lazy, unhurried movements, slow and deep. After several long seconds, I feel her mouth smile against mine. We separate, and I lower my forehead to hers.

She touches her lips as though they're still buzzing from our kiss and takes a step back. "We're doing that again tomorrow, right?"

"Oh, yeah." She pulls away and grins as she walks backward toward the front door of her father's house.

"Good. That's good." Scarlett hops up the steps of her porch and stops with her hand on the front door knob. "Goodnight, Tucker."

"Night, Scarlett."

Her beautiful smile is the last thing I see before she slips through the front door. It's impossible to keep from smiling as I turn and head back across our yards.

"Tucker?"

I turn around to find Alexis shutting the front door. She pulls the strap of her purse farther onto her shoulder and steps off the porch.

"Hey, Lexi. It was really nice of you to let Scarlett have the night off."

"She deserved it. I didn't realize you two were going to spend the evening together."

"Neither did I. It was sort of last-minute."

She nods and looks away for a beat before her eyes pull back to mine. "So, the two of you are a thing now?"

"You know…" I scratch my head. "I don't really know what we are."

"Well, judging by the lip-lock a second ago, you're something."

"You saw that, huh?"

"Couldn't miss it. You two were practically humping in the front yard."

I laugh. "That's a little dramatic."

"I know it's none of my business, but I don't want to see you get hurt, so I'm going to say it anyway. You need to be careful with her. Don't get too comfortable."

Her words leave a sour taste in my mouth for many different reasons. "She's not going to hurt me."

"I wouldn't be so sure about that. This is temporary, Tucker. She's here until Dad gets better. Her friends aren't here, her home isn't here, her life isn't here."

I know that she's right, but I'll be damned if Scarlett's actions don't speak differently. "I appreciate the concern, but I can take care of myself."

"Of course, you can. I wasn't trying to imply that you couldn't, It's just—you know what? Never mind."

Lexi pulls her keys from her purse and unlocks her car.

Go back inside, Tucker, just walk away. But I can't. I know it's none of my business, but I hate the way that Lexi views her sister.

"Whatever anger you're holding onto, Lexi, you need to let it go."

Her head pops up. "Excuse me?"

"You've got a chip on your shoulder when it comes to Scarlett. Yes, she screwed up, but she's tried to make it right over the years. Did you ever thank her for the car she bought you? Or the year's worth of housekeeping she paid for? Or what about the time she bought every item off your baby registry?"

Even in the dark, I can see her face pale. "How did you know about all of that?"

"Rick told me."

"Of course, he did. He's always bragging about Scarlett."

"He brags about you too, you're just not around when he does it. It's not a competition. She's your sister, Lexi, and she loves you. Cut her some slack. Have you even brought the kids over here to see her since she's been home?"

Tears shimmer in Lexi's eyes as she shakes her head. "No, but they've been asking to see her."

"Then what are you waiting for?"

"I don't want her to leave them the way she left me."

"It's been twelve years. She's not the same person she once was. Give her a chance, Lexi. She can't prove you wrong if you don't give her a chance."

"Is that what you're doing, giving her a chance and hoping that she proves you wrong?"

"She has nothing to prove when it comes to me."

Because I have no control when it comes to her.

10

~SCARLETT~

"Whoa."

"What?" Dad asks, looking down at his nice, blue polo shirt and khaki shorts. "Did I drop something on myself?"

"No, you look really nice," I reply and stand to straighten his collar. "What are you all dressed up for?"

Before he can answer, the doorbell rings.

"Hold that thought." I hurry over to the front door and find Tucker standing on the other side. He's in a sharp green button-down with jeans that hug his thighs perfectly. He shuffles back and forth on his cowboy boots.

And he's holding flowers.

"Dad, your date's here."

Tucker's eyes dance with humor as he steps inside.

"He's not *my* date," Dad says with a laugh.

"What's going on?" I ask, tilting my head to the side and hooking a loose strand of hair behind my ear.

"These are for you," Tucker says, holding the arrangement of red poppies and purple lilacs in my direction. "And I'm taking you out on the town this evening."

"Is Dad coming with us?" I raise a brow and look back at my father, who's currently smiling like the Cheshire Cat.

"Nah, I've got poker night," Dad replies.

"And Chloe's at a friend's house for the night." Tucker leans against the door and grins at me. "So, we have the whole evening to ourselves."

"Poker? Dad, are you sure that's a good idea?"

"I had a stroke, I'm not dead. I'll be here at home—my walker within reach—and the guys will be here if I need something. Go on your date, and don't worry about me."

"But..." I look down at my cut-off shorts and dirty tank top. "I've been scrubbing bathrooms," I inform Tucker. "I'm in no shape to go out right now."

"You've got thirty minutes," Tucker replies, his eyes sweeping up and down my body, leaving gooseflesh in the wake of his gaze. "And then you're mine."

"Thirty minutes?" I laugh and shake my head. "I need at least an hour."

"Thirty," Tucker repeats, his voice strong, leaving no room for argument. He's gazing at me with lust and manly affection, and I can't resist him.

"I'd better hurry."

I rush up the stairs to my room, excited about my impromptu date, and strip out of my clothes. A decade of concerts with more costume changes than a girl can shake a stick at has come in surprisingly handy for this occasion.

I'm in and out of the shower in five minutes. Thankfully, I washed my hair last night, so all I have to do is use the blow-dryer and a big brush to tame my long locks. At the halfway point of my allotted time, I brush on some makeup and hurry to the closet.

This is going to be the hard part. What the hell do I wear? I wish I had my full wardrobe back in Tennessee to work with. Sure, Tuck's always just been a friend, but we're much more than that now, and I want to look my best.

I'll ponder the whole *more* thought later. There's no time right now.

It's warm out this evening, so I settle on a pretty summer dress. It's pink, flowy, and falls off one shoulder.

With one last look in the mirror, I slip on some brown sandals and hurry downstairs.

"Twenty-eight minutes," I say triumphantly. "That's a record."

Tucker's eyes are pinned to me, and his jaw drops. The lust in his eyes has me squeezing my thighs together. *This man is lethal.*

"You sure look nice, sugar," Dad says as he plants a kiss on my cheek. "Now, you two have fun tonight. Be careful. Be *safe*, if you know what I mean."

"Dad."

"Do you have condoms?" he asks Tucker, pulling him out of the apparent lusty fog he's been in. "Because if not, I might have some—"

"Oh my God, Dad." I cover my ears and close my eyes. "Stop talking."

Tucker wraps his arm around my waist, pulling me against him. "We're good to go."

"All right, then. Have fun, you two." Dad smiles smugly. "I just want to say, I told you so."

"Goodnight," I say, narrowing my eyes at my father. "Wait, we can't leave until your friends get here. What time are they coming?"

We hear a car door slam.

"Sounds like right now," Dad says. "Don't come home before midnight. We play pretty late, and no women allowed."

"So noted," I mumble, feeling frazzled as Tucker guides me down the porch steps toward his car in his driveway.

"Hi, Miss Scarlett," Ray Howard calls with a wave. "Thanks for letting us borrow your daddy tonight."

"Have fun!" I wave back and climb into Tucker's car. "I haven't seen Ray since I was a kid."

"He and your dad are close," Tucker says with a nod and pulls away from the house. "Rick will be well taken care of tonight."

"How long have you been planning this?"

"A few days." He glances at me and grins. His face is freshly shaven, and I can't resist reaching out to brush my fingertips down his cheek. He takes my hand in his and kisses my knuckles before resting our linked hands on his leg.

"Where are we going?"

"Are you hungry?" he asks.

"I'm always hungry."

He nods. "How does Mama Italiana sound?"

"Delicious."

I settle back against the seat and watch our little town pass by. It's changed so much. Grown dramatically. So much so that I barely recognize it.

"When did that little strip mall go in?"

"About ten years ago."

New Hope is charming. A river runs right through it, with huge oak trees flanking it on either side. It's perfect for picnics and parties.

"Looks like they paved those walking paths by the river."

"A few years ago, yeah. It's great for running, walking, biking. You name it."

"I like it."

He squeezes my hand and pulls into Mama's. It's a Friday evening, so the lot is full. Mama's makes the best lasagna in the state and has been a hotspot in town for three decades.

"It's good to see that some things haven't changed."

"Like the food?"

"Exactly. It wouldn't be home without Charlie's and Mama's."

Tucker walks around the car to open my door, takes my hand, and leads me into the restaurant. The tables are covered in red-and-white-checkered tablecloths. The room is dimly lit, with candles stuck in wine bottles on every table.

"Hi, Mr. Tucker," a pretty young woman says with a bright smile when she sees us. "I have your table ready."

"Thanks, Shelly."

She preens and leads us through the packed restaurant to a

table in the back. I notice that people see us, recognize us, but no one says a thing to me.

Tucker, on the other hand, is a different story. People wave, or call out, "hey there, Tucker." He smiles and waves back as we weave our way through the tables.

This is new for me. I'm usually the one everyone wants to say hello to, wants to hug and have their photo taken with.

But tonight, in our hometown, Tucker's the celebrity. I might as well be invisible.

I don't know how to feel about that.

"I'll sit next to you, if you don't mind," Tucker says, sliding into the booth next to me, rather than across from me.

"I don't mind."

"Here you go," Shelly says, passing us laminated menus, and then, after giving Tucker another big smile, showing off a dimple in her left cheek, she sashays away.

"I don't even have to look at it," Tucker says, setting his menu aside. "I get the same thing every time."

I glance over the menu, surprised to see that nothing on it has changed since I left town. "I guess I'm the same."

I lay my menu on top of his, and just as he leans in to whisper something in my ear, a woman approaches the table.

She glances at me, but she's all about Tucker as she touches his shoulder and smiles.

"I wanted to come over to say thank you again for stopping by the other night. I don't know what I would've done without you."

She winks at him, her hand still resting on his shoulder, and I feel my eyes narrow on her.

He was at her house? What did he do for her, exactly?

I'm not used to feeling jealous. At all.

I'm not a jealous woman.

But I don't like this.

"Just doing my job," Tucker replies, then turns back to me, dismissing the blonde. She smiles and awkwardly turns away. "You look amazing," he whispers in my ear.

"Thanks. I didn't have a lot of time to get ready. Who was that?"

"Maryanne Thompson. Her cat was stuck in a tree."

"That's a little cliché, isn't it?"

She probably put her pet in the tree on purpose. Poor thing.

Tucker shrugs and kisses the spot below my ear, causing me to shiver. "I just responded to the call."

"Isn't that something a firefighter would normally take care of?" I ask, tilting my head a little to the side so he has more room to keep kissing me.

"The department was already on a call. Are you jealous?"

"No," I scoff, shaking my head. "I don't get jealous. It's not part of my DNA."

"Good." His hand slides over my thigh, and through the thin material of my dress, I can feel his warmth. All thoughts of Maryanne and her cat fly right out the window. "I haven't been able to stop thinking about you since our kiss."

I drag in a ragged breath and look around. We're in a corner, and no one is paying us any attention. There sure as heck isn't any paparazzi around, and the tablecloth reaches the floor.

I part my legs, allowing his hand to drop between them.

Tucker's eyes fly to mine, a mischievous grin on his handsome face. "You always were a little wild."

"Not much has changed."

"That's where you're wrong," he whispers, capturing my lips in another kiss. "Everything has changed."

His hand inches higher and higher, lifting my dress with its ascent, and... *Oh, God. Come on, Tucker, just do it already.*

I'm so freaking turned on. If we weren't in a busy restaurant, I'd climb on top of him and take over.

"Tucker Andrews, is that you?"

Seriously? We're interrupted, again, this time by a brunette with big, brown eyes and fake boobs bigger than Dolly's.

"Hey, Darla."

Dolly, Darla. Darla, Dolly. Close enough.

The difference is, I adore Dolly. She's always been nothing but sweet to me. Writing *Whiskey and Roses* with her three years ago was one of the biggest honors of my life.

Darla, however, can take a long walk off a short pier. How dare she think it's okay to just walk up and interrupt two people when they're...okay, so maybe she didn't exactly know what she was interrupting. But, still. It's rude.

And something that happens to me all the damn time, which is why I sit back and take a deep breath.

"I can't remember the last time I've seen you out of your uniform. You're usually always on duty. Casual looks good on you." Darla props her hands on her hips, showcasing her impressive breasts, and really, I want to laugh.

But I'm not a mean girl.

I am, however, a little territorial, and she needs to step back.

"He surprised me with a night out," I say, taking Tuck's hand in mine. I kiss his shoulder and smile up at her. "Isn't that sweet?"

Darla's smile falters as she looks at our hands. "Well, well, well, if it isn't Scarlett Kincaid. I heard you were in town."

I tilt my head to the side. "I'm sorry, I don't believe we've met. Are you from around here?"

She nods smugly and licks her lips as her eyes fall to Tucker. "Born and raised, but you probably don't remember me from school. I'm quite a bit younger than you."

"Ah. Well, I'm sure there are men your own age around here somewhere. Now, if you don't mind, we'd like to get back to our date."

I smile innocently, and Darla scowls, looking at Tucker to save her.

"It was nice seeing you, Darla. Enjoy your evening," he says, dismissing her in the nicest possible way.

Her jaw drops, and then she huffs away.

"You don't get jealous, huh? Your brown eyes are looking a bit green, sweetheart."

I shrug my bare shoulder. "I mean, I'm sitting *right here*. They can flirt with you when I'm not around."

He kisses my temple just as our waitress arrives.

"Hey, Tucker. Scarlett." She pulls a pad of paper out of the pocket on her apron. "What can I get y'all tonight?"

"Lasagna, extra bread," I inform her, fully intending to spend the morning working out to burn off the extra carbs.

"Two of those," Tucker says.

"Drinks?"

"Two sweet teas," Tucker replies before I can respond, and then the waitress is gone, weaving her way through the full tables. "You don't have anything to be jealous of."

"I told you, I'm not jealous," I lie easily, sipping my water.

"No. Not at all." He laughs and wraps an arm around my shoulders, tugging me closer to him. "You're the poster child for calm and collected."

"I know."

He laughs now and kisses my cheek. Affectionate Tucker is new. He wasn't this handsy when he was seventeen. Then again... I didn't give him the chance to be.

I like it.

A lot.

"You have good hands," I inform him, running my fingers over his knuckles.

"Keep touching me like that, and I'll have to show you just how *good* they can be," he breathes, and the entire room falls away, leaving just the two of us.

It's like something out of a cheesy chick flick, and I love it more than I can say. My heart pounds, my breaths coming fast as I stare up into his eyes, wishing he would kiss me and touch me.

Because Tucker can *kiss*.

"Tucker..." In a brazen move, I take his hand and put it back on my thigh.

"Here ya go," the waitress says as she sets our plates in front of us.

Really? I blow out a breath, and Tucker laughs. He's enjoying this. He knows that I'm absolutely crazy for him, and he's getting a kick out of my frustration.

"That was quick," I say.

"Lasagna and bread is pretty easy." She winks, sets our teas on the table, then hurries away.

"I'm starving," I say, trying to calm my libido. Plus, the faster we eat, the quicker we can get out of here.

"Me, too," he replies. But his eyes aren't on our delicious meal, they're on me. My body heats under his stare, and I nudge him with my arm.

"Food will have to do for now, I guess."

"Lightning bugs." I point ahead on the path where the insects bob and weave through the air.

"You always had a soft spot for them. Wouldn't let me catch them."

"You used to pull their lights off," I say, remembering the days we spent running together down by the river.

One evening, Tucker pulled a light from a lightning bug and stuck it on my ring finger. "It looks like a diamond on your hand," he said, proud of what he'd done.

"Ew, get that off me." I wiped my finger off in the grass and scowled at Tucker. "You just killed an innocent bug to put a gross green light on my finger."

"Next time I put something on your finger, it'll be a ring," was his reply. Tucker wasn't a cocky sixteen-year-old, but he knew what he wanted, and he wanted me. Unfortunately, I was a bitch of epic proportions, and the only thing I had my eye on was getting the hell out of dodge.

"In your dreams, Tucker Andrews."

"What are you thinking about?" Tucker asks, pulling me from the memory.

"Us."

"I like that topic. What about us?"

After dinner, we decided to wander by the river, hand in hand. The sexual tension between us has been off the charts. Part of me wishes we'd gone right home to get naked and sweaty.

The other part of me is happy for this reprieve. Things are moving fast between us. I don't regret it—at all—but once we do this, there's no going back. We'll officially cross the line from childhood buddies to lovers, and I admit, I'm a bit nervous.

I'm *not* second-guessing. There's a difference.

When I'm around Tucker, my body feels like a live wire, and when he touches me, I light up. Just the thought of him being on top of me, feeling the weight of his body as he devours me, has me sucking in a sharp breath.

"Are you feeling okay? I can take you home if you're not," he offers, looking a little disappointed at the prospect.

"I can't go home," I remind him. "No women allowed, remember?"

He grins. "Pretty sure your dad wouldn't kick you out."

"I don't want to go home."

We stop on the sidewalk by his car. He grips my shoulders and turns me to face him. His eyes shine in the moonlight. His jaw is firm and tight, his hands warm.

He's home for me. He always has been.

"I don't want to go to my dad's house. I want to go home with you."

"There's nothing I would love more than to take you back to my place. But, Scarlett, you look nervous." He presses a hand over the left side of my chest. "Your heart is beating a mile a minute, and your cheeks are flushed. Sweetheart, we don't have to do anything you're not ready for." He drags a knuckle down the apple of my cheek. "We're in no hurry, Scar."

"I don't have jitters. I'm no virgin, Tuck, any more than you are. That's just what you do to me. Being close to you makes my heart race."

He smiles. "Nothing else is bothering you, then?"

"Maybe one thing." He cups my cheek, and I close my hand over his, leaning into his touch. "I don't want to lose our friendship. If something happens, and we don't work out, I don't want to lose you again. I just got you back."

He steps closer and lowers his face to within inches of mine.

"I'm not going anywhere. Whether we go home and make love all night, or you tell me to back the hell off, I'm your friend, Scarlett."

I don't deserve him. I don't deserve this tenderness, this loyalty.

But I won't reject it. I didn't know how much I missed this, missed *him* until I had him back in my life again, and I will *not* fuck this up.

"Now what are you thinking?"

"I'm thinking that it's about time you take me back to your place and have your way with me."

"Oh, yeah?"

"Yeah. What're you thinking?" *Please tell me you're thinking the same thing.*

"I'm thinking that you're the most beautiful woman I've ever seen."

"I like it. Keep going."

"And I'm the luckiest man in the world because I'm here with you."

"Tuck?"

"Yes, sweetness."

"Take me home before I get you naked on the hood of your car."

"Yes, ma'am."

11

~ TUCKER ~

BEING around Scarlett is a continuous struggle. Even more so as an adult than when I was a teenager. She's so gorgeous and sweet and funny and sassy, and all I want to do when she's around is shove her up against a wall and bury myself deep inside her body.

Dinner tonight was torture. When she spread her legs beneath the table, I thought I was going to come right there in my pants like a horny virgin teenager. I struggled to keep it together throughout dinner, and now I'm fighting to keep my cock deflated until we get back to my place, which is practically impossible with her sitting beside me in that dress.

I wasn't lying when I told her that she's the most beautiful woman I've ever seen—she truly is. But it's not just what's on the outside that I find attractive. All of Scarlett is sexy, even the green monster she keeps hidden deep inside.

I pull into the driveway, open her car door, and we practically run like school kids to the front door. She wraps herself around me, peppering me with kisses while I try to unlock the door. We stumble through it in a tangle of arms and legs, and as soon as I get the door shut, I spin her around and pin her against it.

The smile on her face dies. Her eyes fall to my lips. I push my fingers into her hair, cup the back of her head, and pull her face toward mine. Our lips crash together. A low moan pulls from her throat, and that's all the encouragement I need. I push my tongue into her mouth and kiss her the way I've been dreaming about since our make-out session in her dad's front yard.

She fists the front of my shirt and plasters her soft curves to my body, and there's no holding back the groan that pulls from my chest. I've dreamed of this for years—having her all to myself. Now, here she is, my sweet Scarlett, trying to climb me like a tree.

With one hand on her head, keeping her where I want her, I slide the other to her lower back. I press my palm to the small dip at the top of her ass and she arches, pushing her hips to mine. When she rolls her hips against me, I cup a hand to her ass and lift her up.

Scarlett wraps her legs around my waist. Her hands are everywhere—in my hair, sliding over my shoulders and along my neck before diving back into my hair. I could've taken her against the door, but I've waited too damn long to be with this woman, and I want to do it right.

With our lips fused together, I stride down the hall and kick open my bedroom door. I lower Scarlett to her feet and take a step back. Her chest rises and falls with each ragged breath she takes. Her lips are swollen and red, her eyes hooded, and all I want to do is drink her in, memorize everything about this moment because everything about it is perfect. But Scarlett has other plans. She launches herself at me.

She whispers my name before her lips land on mine. Our tongues stroke each other in desperation, our hands reaching and pulling and holding on with more passion than I've ever felt. But if we don't slow things down, I'm going to embarrass myself.

Pulling my mouth from hers, I skim my lips across her jaw and down the side of her neck. "Slow down, baby. We're in no hurry."

"I can't slow down. I need you, Tucker."

"You have me."

She growls. "You know what I mean."

I chuckle against her skin. "I never could say no to you."

I bring my hands to her neck and slowly slide them down her shoulders, pulling her dress down until the material pools in a pile at our feet. My eyes rake over her body, devouring her as she stands before me in a strapless nude lace bra and matching panties.

"My God, you're beautiful."

"Tucker."

When I look up, our eyes meet. Hers are full of hunger as she searches my face.

"Slow first, or fast? You choose, but make no mistake about it, at some point tonight, I'm taking my time and learning every inch of your body," I declare, grazing my knuckles over her chest. My eyes follow the movement of my hand, and when I brush them along her stomach, she quivers. I trail my finger along the edge of her underwear. "What's it going to be?"

Her nipples peak against the lacy material, and my mouth waters, but I won't taste her until she gives me an answer.

"Fast," she replies, arousal thick in her voice.

I flatten my hand on her stomach and smooth it upward between her breasts. I unclip the front clasp of her bra and watch it fall from her body. The rush of cool air causes her nipples to pucker even tighter under my stare. Her head drops forward. She watches me stroke her breasts softly.

"This isn't fast." Her breath hitches on the last word when I pinch the tight peak between my thumb and forefinger. "*Oh, God.* Please, Tucker, hurry. I just want you inside of me."

Fuck. Those words from her mouth would bring any man to his knees.

"Get on the bed and spread your legs."

Her eyes stay locked on mine as she positions herself in the center of my mattress, not shy in the least. Scarlett's breasts are perfectly round—not too big, not too small, with dusky nipples that beg for my mouth. There's a softness to her stomach that has me aching to feel her body beneath mine. Slowly, she spreads her legs, and my eyes are drawn to the damp material between them.

"You're soaked."

"That's what you do to me. All I can think about is having you inside of me. It's making me crazy."

I unbutton my shirt and toss it on the floor, and then I reach back and pull my undershirt over my head. Her eyes drop to my zipper, her lips parting as I pull my jeans and boxers off and kick them aside.

My erection bobs heavily in front of me. She smirks and teases one of her breasts with her fingers before dipping lower. She hooks her thumbs in the sides of her panties and inches them down her thighs before wiggling out of them.

This woman is going to be the death of me.

With a knee on the mattress, I inch toward her. I slide my body down to the bed, push her thighs open, and bury my face between her legs. Scarlett bucks her hips, pressing her core against my face.

"Oh, fuck," she hisses, dropping her head against the pillow.

"Eyes on me, sweetheart," I encourage, pushing a finger inside of her. "I want you to watch me when my mouth is on you."

Her hooded eyes find mine. She pushes up on her elbows and looks down at me cradled between her legs.

"That's it, baby." I pump my fingers several times before pulling them out and rubbing a tight circle around her clit. She grinds against my hand, undoubtedly searching for more. With a thumb pressed to her clit, I slide two fingers deep inside her body. "Tell me how it feels, Scarlett. Tell me what you want."

Her eyes widen. Judging by the look on her face, no man has ever pushed her like this in the bedroom.

"Tell me what you want, and I'll give it to you."

"I want your mouth on me. Suck my cli—" Her words morph into a moan when I do exactly what she asks. I keep my fingers inside of her, stroking until the spot I was looking for begins to swell.

I thrust my hips against the bed, searching for any amount of friction as her body comes to life beneath my touch. In a matter of seconds, she explodes. Her thighs clench tightly around my head, her body shuddering as she cries out.

My name falls from her lips in a mangled, drawn-out sigh. When her clit stops pulsing, I ease my hand from her body, situate myself higher up on the bed, and pull her into my arms. I hold her to me, stroking a hand over her hair and down her back as her breathing slows. Eventually, she looks up at me and smiles.

"You're really good at that."

"It's you. I'm good at that because it's you." I run a thumb along her lower lip, and she nips playfully at it. "Watching you fall apart was the sexiest thing I've ever witnessed."

"I bet I can top that." Scarlett swings a leg over my hips and straddles me. Her hair falls forward, wrapping us in our own little cocoon as she leans forward and kisses me.

Warm, soft lips travel down my neck and over my pec, and when she kisses my stomach, the soft, gentle touch causes my abs to ripple.

"Baby, I don't think I can handle that right now," I say, hooking my hands under her arms so I can drag her back up my body.

"I've never really enjoyed going down on a man, but with you, I want to," she pouts.

I nip at her bottom lip. "And I'll let you later. But right now, I'm going to fuck you so hard, sink so deep inside of you, that you'll have a permanent ache between your legs."

Scarlett squeals when I wrap an arm around her back and flip us over so that I'm hovering above her. She reaches between us and wraps her hand around my cock as I lean down to kiss her. I love the taste of her, the feel of her body beneath mine. I'll never get this woman out of my system.

"I'm on the pill," she says breathlessly while guiding me to her entrance. "I can't wait."

Our lips collide, biting, licking, nipping. One thrust of my hips and I'm seated inside of her, deeper than I ever thought possible.

Scarlett cries out in pleasure, her nails scoring my back. Everything about her overwhelms me. Every breath, every kiss, every touch, she's all-consuming, and I press my hips to hers and hold them there while I try to regain some sort of composure.

She lifts her hips, trying to get me to move, but I still her with a hand to her waist. "Wait," I say hoarsely. "Give me a minute. I've wanted this for so long, thought about it so much, and you feel so fucking good wrapped around me."

Her muscles clamp around my cock, and I shake my head. "Do that again, and I won't last."

She does it again and laughs when I nip the spot beneath her ear.

"That's what I'm going for. You're so thick inside of me, stretching me, and I want to feel more of you."

My control snaps. I slide a hand up her thigh, hook her leg around my back, and thrust into her again. Her lids flutter closed, but she quickly opens her eyes as though she knows it's something I'll demand of her.

Good girl.

Scarlett holds on tight, her nails scratching my back, biting into my ass as I pound into her over and over, pushing her further and further into the mattress. The sounds of our labored breathing and flesh meeting fills the air, pushing me toward the proverbial edge.

I push a hand between our sweaty bodies, press my thumb to her clit, and rub. Two tight circles and she flies apart. The strangled moan and look of pleasure on her face pushes me over the edge. Electricity races down my spine, settling between my legs. My muscles strain and flex as I let out a guttural moan. Our bodies spasm and shudder as I collapse against her.

I press my lips to the base of her neck and breathe her in. "Do you know how many times I've thought about being here with you like this?"

She shakes her head and cups my face. There's an unexpected tremble to her hands.

"Are you okay?" I ask.

"Better than okay."

"You're shaking."

"Adrenaline. Emotion. You."

"All good things," I say, brushing my lips across hers.

"All great things." She smiles softly. "Please tell me we're going to do that again."

"Give me two minutes, and I'll be ready for round two," I say, my dick already twitching inside of her.

"Can we make it three? I need to use the restroom."

I roll off of her, and she jumps from the bed. "Do you want something to drink?" I ask.

"A water would be great."

I smack her bare ass, and she giggles as she disappears into the bathroom. I saunter into the kitchen, grab a bottle of water, twist off the top, and chug half of it. I grab another bottle, and by the time I make it back to the bedroom, Scarlett is sprawled out in all of her naked glory.

Her eyes drop to my cock, which grows impossibly hard beneath her heated stare.

"Tucker?"

"Yeah."

She spreads her legs and slips a finger between her wet folds. "I'm not so thirsty anymore."

"Thank fuck." I drop the bottles and climb onto the bed.

"Oh, no," she says, pushing me onto my back so she can straddle me. "This time, I'm on top."

I fold my arms behind my head and smile up at her. "Do your worst."

Scarlett edges herself along my cock, driving me out of my mind— There's a loud knock on the front door.

"Scarlett, it's me, Phillip," a guy yells.

Scarlett's eyes grow round. "Is that Phillip McCormick?" she whispers, referring to one of her dad's friends.

I nod and slide my hand along her waist before cupping her breast because I can't resist her when she's sitting on me, naked.

"I know you're in there because we saw you guys run in the house a while ago," he yells loud enough for us to hear him down the hall.

Scarlett laughs and drops her head to my shoulder.

"Anyway, just wanted to let you know that we're leaving, and your dad is going to bed. He said to tell you to take your time. No rush. He also said that he hopes you had fun but wants me to remind you to be safe. Okay, well, I hope you heard me. I'm gonna go now."

I laugh.

Scarlett groans. "Kill me now."

"I can fuck you now."

"That'll work."

12

~SCARLETT~

How in the ever-loving hell am I supposed to get back in the sexy-time mood after my dad's bestie just yelled at us through the damn door?

"Maybe I should head home," I say, biting my lip and staring down at the sexiest man I've seen in, well...ever.

"If Rick's in bed, you don't have to hurry." Tucker's hand roams from my hip and up over my ribs to my breast. He lazily plucks at the already hard nipple, and I close my eyes with a soft sigh. "We haven't gotten to the whole *slow* portion of this program."

"We wouldn't want to skip that."

He grins and sits up, wrapping his arms around me. "No, we definitely can't skip it."

He palms my ass and lifts me gently until the head of his cock finds my throbbing pussy. I slowly sink over him, taking him as deeply as I can.

"You're amazing," he whispers against my lips. "So much better than any fantasy. You take my breath away."

I bury my fingers in his hair and kiss him softly, gently circling my hips. The friction is slight but no less incredible than what we did just minutes ago. When the tension builds, I drop my head back, and Tucker's mouth finds my neck, kissing and licking, sending even *more* electricity through every damn nerve ending on my body.

"I can't," I whisper. "It's too much."

"Never." His voice is like sandpaper, rough and sexy as hell. He nips at my collarbone, and I bear down, ripples already pulsing through my core. "Jesus, Scar, yes. Fuck, yes."

My body is all raw sensation as I succumb to the orgasm that moves through me like a freaking freight train. Tucker pushes up, *hard,* and growls with his own release.

We're a sweaty, panting heap, staring into each other's eyes as the world comes back into focus around us. He cups my cheek and kisses me, softly at first, and then with more urgency as if he's afraid I'm going to disappear and he's memorizing me completely.

Which is ridiculous because now that I've found *this,* not to mention *him,* I plan to do this as often as possible for however long we can.

"Are you okay?" he asks as he pulls away.

"I am bold enough to say I don't know if I've ever been better," I reply with a grin and brush his hair off his forehead.

"That's a lofty statement coming from a woman with a shelf full of Grammys."

I laugh as he gently rolls us to our sides, facing each other on the bed.

"Exactly. I'm *that* good. How about you?"

"I'm the luckiest man in the world." He sighs and drags his fingertips down my arm. The man can't stop touching me, and I'm not complaining.

"You say some pretty sweet things."

"I don't say anything I don't mean." He kisses my forehead and sighs.

"As much as I'd like to stay here all night—"

"You have to get home to your dad." He nods. "I know."

We reluctantly roll out of bed, and I pull my dress over my head, step into my panties, and slide my feet into my sandals.

Tucker just pulls on an old pair of sweats that hang low on his hips, barely covering the good stuff.

"You expect me to leave when you look like *that*?"

He laughs, tugging me to him for a long kiss. "Trust me, I'd rather keep you here. But you'd better go check on Rick."

"I'm sure he's sleeping." I yawn. "And you've worn me out, too."

"Good." He leads me to the front door and out onto the porch. "I'll stand here and make sure you get home okay."

"It's almost one in the morning in New Hope, South Carolina," I remind him, speaking low. I don't want to wake the neighbors. "What could happen to me in the span of roughly thirty feet?"

He simply leans on the railing and crosses his arms over his bare chest, watching me with a happy grin.

"Fine." I shrug and saunter across the grass, sashaying my hips back and forth for his benefit. When I reach the top of the steps of Dad's porch, I turn back and blow him a kiss.

He catches the imaginary kiss with his hand and presses it to his heart. And just like that, I feel myself go all gooey inside.

Is it possible that I'm falling in love with Tucker Andrews?

I open the front door and walk inside. Dad left the kitchen light on for me, and I walk that way, ready for a bottle of water, but when I step inside, I gasp.

"Daddy!"

"I had a bit of a fall," my father says. He's sitting on the floor, his back against the lower cabinets. "I couldn't get back up, but don't worry, I called Lexi."

"Oh my God, Dad." I squat next to him, looking him over. He's in his pajamas and is missing one of his slippers.

"I tripped on this damn mat."

"Why didn't you call me?"

"You were with Tucker. I didn't want to interrupt you."

"I'm calling the paramedics."

"Just help me up, Scarlett. I'll be fine."

"Do you hurt anywhere?"

"My wrist is a bit sore where I caught myself," he admits. "But I'm fine. It's just my pride that's a bit bruised, that's all."

"No, I'm absolutely calling the paramedics."

Jesus, my heart is hammering so hard in my chest, it's a wonder Tucker can't hear it. I reach for my phone and call 911. Once the call is made, and the ambulance is on the way, I sit on the floor with Dad and hold his hand.

"I don't want to move you in case you've injured something."

"Scarlett, I love you."

"I love you, too."

"But you are the most stubborn person I've ever met. You're causing a fuss for nothing."

"No, I'm not," I insist. The next ten minutes are a blur as the ambulance arrives, and four men come rushing inside with a gurney and all kinds of equipment.

Most of them know my father, and they chat with him, keeping him at ease as they check him out.

"How long have you had this bruise on your knee?" One of them asks my father, making him frown.

"Oh, I must have gotten that when I fell."

"We're going to take you to the emergency room, just to have your wrist and knee looked at," the paramedic named Jimmy says. "I know that's not how you planned to spend your Friday night, but it's really for the best, Mr. Rick."

"Thank you," I say before Dad can complain. I follow them out of the house, just as Lexi is hurrying out of her car and rushing up to meet us. "Lexi, I was just about to call—"

"What the hell is going on?" she demands, her face white as she approaches Dad on the gurney. "Dad, are you okay?"

"I'm fine," he assures her. "I had a little fall, and Scarlett is just being cautious by calling in the troops."

"What did you do?" Lexi rounds on me, pushing her face to mine. "You have *one* job, Scar. Watch Dad, make sure he's safe and well taken care of."

"He had poker night, and I went out with Tucker—"

"This is so you," Lexi interrupts with a humorless laugh. "You let someone else take care of your responsibilities while you go off whoring with *him*."

She points behind me, and I turn, surprised to see Tucker walking up behind me.

"Watch yourself, Alexis," Tucker says, his voice and eyes hard.

"It's true," she insists.

"They're loading him," I say, pulling out of Tucker's grasp as he takes my hand in his. "I'm going with him."

"The hell you are," Lexi says, but I'm already climbing into the ambulance, and the doors are shut before Lexi can say anything more or try to join us. I take Dad's uninjured hand in mine and watch out the back window as Tucker and my sister fade from view.

"She's just upset," Dad says. "She'll cool off."

I smile down at him because I don't want to upset him, but when it comes down to it, Lexi isn't wrong. It *is* my job to take care of our father, and instead, I spent the evening with Tucker. I even stayed after I knew that Dad was home alone, and that's on me.

This is all my fault.

I need to refocus and remember what's most important: my father, not my libido.

"Hey, Dad, are you and Gretchen okay?"

"We're fine, honey," Gretchen says, waving me off. She's Dad's in-home physical therapist. "Rick's all mine for another ninety minutes."

"I'll be back well before then," I assure them both before walking out the back door. I saw Tucker in his garage a little while ago, and I figure now's a good time to go talk with him.

Not that there's ever a good time to have this conversation, but Dad's with Gretchen, and I don't think Chloe's home from her friend's house yet.

Last night was simply relentless. That's the only word I have for it. My emotions were all over the place. I had the best sex of my life with a man I respect and *like*, who I trust wants to be with me for all the right reasons and not just because I'm Scarlett Kincaid, international superstar.

But then I had the terror of finding Dad on the floor, and everything that happened after. To say it was a rollercoaster would be the understatement of the friggin' year.

I hear clanging coming from Tuck's garage, and when I come around to the big door and find it open with Tuck sitting on the floor beside his lawnmower, my stomach takes a dive to my feet.

Dear sweet Lord in Heaven, the man is gorgeous.

He's sweaty, and a little dirty, thanks to the tinkering and the oppressively hot South Carolina summer weather. And when he looks up at me, his eyes narrow.

"How's Rick?"

"He's home. With the physical therapist now, actually."

"Wanna tell me what happened?"

I swallow and nod, not at all happy with the distance in his voice, which makes me a complete asshole because I'm about to tell him I can't see him anymore.

"When I got home last night, I found him on the kitchen floor. He'd fallen sometime after Phillip left and before I got there. I panicked and called the ambulance."

"But you didn't call me."

I tip my head to the side, watching him. "Well, no. It happened really fast, and I was just worried about Dad."

He nods once, using a wrench thingy on the mower. "Go on."

"Well, you saw most of the rest." I twist my hands at my waist, more nervous than I've been in a long time. "We went to the hospital, and they x-rayed the wrist and knee. He didn't break anything, thank goodness. He's a little sore today, but I think it just scared us all more than anything."

"I'm glad to hear that."

"I also came over because I need to talk to you."

"I figured."

He stands, and with one hand, he whips his shirt over his head and proceeds to wipe his sweaty face with it. My tongue is now permanently stuck to the roof of my mouth.

For the love of Mary and Joseph, the man has abs for days. And I remember how they feel under my fingertips. How they move when he's thrusting in and out of me, and...*why did he take his shirt off?*

He wipes his hands, then walks over to the sink in the corner of the garage and starts to wash them.

With his shirt off.

"I'm listening," he says.

I shake my head, trying to pull myself out of the sexy fog that seeing his bare torso dragged me into.

"Well, I had a lot of time to think last night, and you know, Lexi's not entirely wrong. It *is* my job to look after Daddy. And I really shouldn't be letting myself be all distracted by you and your—" I gesture to his body when he turns to look at me, watching me with hot eyes as he dries his hands on a towel.

"My what?"

"Your sexy ways," I say with a deep sigh. "It's not fair to Dad, and I just think I need to be focused. I need to worry about him and getting him well. I can do other things in my spare time, like write songs and maybe weed the garden or something. I have enough on my plate, Tucker."

"I see." He nods and leans on the workbench, crossing his arms over his bare chest.

"I'm glad you agree." I nod once and turn to leave, but he stops me in my tracks with his next words.

"I don't agree. Everything you just said is complete bullshit."

I spin around. "It is *not* bullshit."

He walks toward me, slowly, his hands curling and uncurling into fists at his sides as he approaches. I step back, but he cages me against the wall, one hand planted next to my head, and the other cupping my cheek.

"I don't believe a word of it." His voice is a hoarse whisper. His eyes are pinned to mine, and I've never been so damn turned on in my life. "I know you're used to dishing out the orders and having everyone bend to your will, but I'm not your employee or your minion, Scarlett. I was buried deep inside you not twelve hours ago, and you know as well as I do that it wasn't a casual fuck for either of us."

"Tuck, I just—"

"I listened to you. Now, it's your turn to listen. You walking out of here and never speaking to me again is *not* how this is going to work. Not today or any other day."

He leans closer and presses his lips to that spot he found last night, the one just under my earlobe. But he doesn't kiss me there. No, he whispers against my skin.

Because I didn't *already* have gooseflesh all up and down my damn body.

"You can be a good daughter *and* be in a relationship, Scar."

"Is that what this is?" My voice sounds breathless to my ears.

"How would you describe it?" He lifts me effortlessly, and with my back propped against the wall, and my legs wrapped around his waist, his thumb makes its way under the hem of my little cut-off shorts and finds my wet panties. "I don't think just anyone does this to you."

"That's just sex," I insist, then moan when he makes light little circles over my clit. Even through the thin material of my panties, it makes me crazy. My nipples immediately pucker, and my legs tighten around him.

"Tell me what you feel is purely physical," he challenges.

"*You* tell *me*." I watch his face, unwilling to be the only vulnerable one in the room.

"I've never felt for *anyone* what I feel for you," he growls. "It's not just the sex, although it's the best fucking sex of my life. I told you last night, *it's you*. You make me laugh and think. I'm so damn proud of you, and yes, you turn me on."

He presses his hard cock against my core, dry humping me against the wall, and I'll be damned…he's about to make me come just like this.

"Tuck," I whimper, cradling his face now. "Damn you, Tucker."

"I'm not letting you do this, Scar. You're not going to walk away from this. You're not going to walk away from *me*, damn it."

"I don't know what to do," I blurt, frustrated beyond belief. "Everything I do is wrong. Lexi reminds me almost daily that what I'm doing for Dad isn't enough. So, I came here to tell you that I can't see you anymore, but that doesn't feel right either."

"Because it's not," he agrees. "You can have both. You don't have to choose between me and your dad, Scar."

I tip my head back against the wall and swallow hard. I don't want to give Tucker up. God, I just found him again, and being with him feels so *right*.

"I have to do right by my dad," I inform him.

"You're already doing all the right things," he reminds me. "Lexi's an angry woman. Don't let her ruin everything for you. You're home, for the first time in a dozen years. *Enjoy* it, baby."

I hug him, wrapping my arms around his neck and holding on for all I'm worth. He feels so damn good against me, but more than that, being with him just feels right. He soothes me in ways I didn't know I needed.

He's my best friend *and* my lover.

And I'm not giving him up. Not for Lexi. Not for anyone.

"Okay," I whisper.

"Trust me." He kisses my cheek sweetly. "You've got this. You're stronger than you give yourself credit for."

I nod and smile down at him, brushing my fingertips down his rough cheek.

"We'll figure it out," I say.

"Oh, yeah. We've got this."

~ TUCKER ~

"WHATCHA COOKIN'?" Dean hollers across the yard.

Scarlett is standing on her dad's deck. There are some seriously delicious smells coming from Rick's grill, and my stomach growls. I should probably think about making something for dinner. Chloe got home from school an hour ago, and she's probably starving. The girl is growing like a weed. She's also trying to eat me out of house and home.

"Burgers." Scarlett lowers the lid of the grill then sets the spatula down and leans a hip against the deck railing. "What are you guys doing?"

"Just hanging out. I'm spending time with my brother and my favorite niece."

"I'm your only niece," Chloe says, giving her uncle Dean a look.

"Then I guess you win by default, huh, kid?" Dean ruffles her hair and laughs when Chloe slaps his hand away.

"I'm not a kid."

"You're telling me," I quip, remembering the tween drama I had to deal with not too long ago.

Chloe rolls her eyes and looks at Scarlett. "Any chance I can have dinner with you and Rick so that I can get away from these two?"

Scarlett laughs. "Come on over."

I love watching Scarlett interact with Chloe. She's so good with her. Natural.

"Yes!" Chloe sticks her tongue out at Dean and runs across the yard. "Thanks, Scarlett."

"You bet. Can you run inside and hang with Dad for a few minutes while I finish up these burgers?"

"Sure." Chloe disappears into the house while Scarlett flips the patties. When she's done, she pulls her hair up into a loose knot on top of her head. The move causes her already short shirt to rise up, revealing her stomach.

Scarlett is gorgeous with curves for days, and one of the things I love most about her is her confidence. She's not stick-thin, her ribs aren't showing, and she's not obsessed with food. She eats what she wants, when she wants, and is comfortable in her own skin.

"You're one lucky bastard, you know that?" Dean whispers, not bothering to hide the fact that he's openly ogling my girlfriend.

Girlfriend.

I like the sound of that. I smile to myself and nod.

"I know."

"Are you two hungry?" Scarlett asks.

Dean nods and rubs his belly. "Starving."

"Well then, get over here." Scarlett waves us over. "I'll throw on some brats and a few more burgers."

"That's it. I'm stealing her." Dean takes a purposeful stride toward Scarlett, and I dart after him.

"The hell you are." He laughs when I knock him out of the way. "Get your own girl."

"But I want yours." I growl. "I'm joking." He laughs, holding up his hands and taking a step back. "I don't think any man in this town would be stupid enough to go after her with you prowling around."

"Smart men."

When we get to Scarlett, I wrap an arm around her waist, pull her close, and kiss her. "Are you sure you don't mind us crashing your dinner?"

"Are you kidding? The more, the merrier. You two watch the grill while I grab some more food."

She walks inside, and Dean lifts the lid to the grill, revealing giant Angus burgers. They've been dipped in barbecue sauce and look mouthwatering.

"She's sexy, smart, funny, successful, and she knows how to grill." Dean shakes his head and whistles low as he shuts the lid. "You hit the fucking jackpot. Better not let this one go."

"I don't plan on it."

"Don't plan on what?" Scarlett says, walking out with a plate of meat.

"Letting you go."

"Good." She smiles, pushing onto her toes to kiss me. "Because I don't think you could get rid of me if you tried."

I'm damn glad to hear that, especially after the shit she tried to pull a few days ago. Honestly, I think she just got scared. All she needed was a gentle reminder that she's doing a good job of taking care of her dad and that we're perfect together. Now, my girl is happy, *I'm* happy, and for the first time in over a decade, all is right in the world.

"Want some help?" I wrap my arms around her stomach and rest my chin on her shoulder. She angles her head so that she can kiss my nose.

"No, thank you. I've got this."

Dean plops down onto a patio chair, but I'm comfortable right where I am, watching Scarlett cook.

"Where did you learn to grill? I assumed you had a chef who cooks for you while you're on tour."

"Oh, I do. Bernard is great."

"He taught you?"

"No." She smiles up at me proudly. "I taught myself."

"When?"

"This morning."

I lift a brow. "This morning?"

"Yep. Don't look so surprised," she says, laughing. "Daddy wanted burgers from the grill for dinner, and I'm not about to let him down again—Lord knows I've done that enough—so, I did a Google search, pulled up a few recipes, and voila!"

"Wow. I'm impressed."

"Let's save the compliments until we taste the food."

"I'm sure it'll be great."

"This is gonna get old fast," Dean mumbles.

"What is?" I ask.

"You two acting lovey-dovey all the time."

Scarlett turns in my arms, wraps hers around my neck, and smiles at Dean before kissing me full on the mouth. Lips, tongue, teeth clacking, the whole nine yards.

Dean gags, and we're interrupted when the back door flies open.

"Oh my God," Chloe screeches. "Ew. Gross. I can't un-see that."

Scarlett pulls back and touches her lips, just as affected by the kiss as I am. Her glossy eyes dart to my daughter, who is making an exaggerated gagging sound.

"What's all the commotion about?" Rick says, walking onto the deck from the house.

Chloe wrinkles her nose and looks at Rick. "Dad and Scarlett were making out."

"Oh, yeah?" Rick looks way too happy. "That's not a bad thing, Chlo."

"I know it's not, but I don't need to see it."

"Remember that when you start dating," I say.

I kiss Scarlett on the side of the head and walk across the deck to pull out a chair for Rick.

"Atta boy," he whispers, giving me a wry smile as he sits down. "I knew you and Scar would end up together."

"Dad, don't—" Scarlett's words taper off. I turn around to see why, and that's when my eyes land on Alexis.

She's walking toward us with the same scowl she's been wearing since Scarlett's return home. A second later, her kids walk around the corner, pushing and shoving at each other, but they perk up at the sight of Scarlett.

"Aunt Scarlett!" they yell in unison, darting across the yard.

Scarlett runs after them, meeting them in the middle and scoops them both into her arms. I can't see her face from where I'm sitting, but I'd bet just about anything that she's fighting back tears.

"I missed you both so much," she says, pulling back so she can look at them. "Look at you guys. You're getting so big."

"I'm bigger," Declan says, puffing out his chest.

Lucy answers him with an elbow to his stomach. "You might be bigger, but I'm older and stronger."

"Stop fighting and go give your grandpa a hug," Alexis says.

Scarlett turns and watches the kids run toward Rick. She swipes a finger under her eye and looks at Alexis, but she doesn't get a word out because Alexis is faster.

"Well, isn't this cozy? A nice little family dinner."

"It wasn't planned. We were all just outside and decided to eat together."

I hate that Scarlett feels the need to defend herself and what's happening. Alexis needs to pull the stick out of her ass and get over whatever grudge she's holding onto.

"Well, the kids and I won't stay long."

"Don't go," Scarlett says. "Stay. Have dinner with us. I can make some hotdogs for the kids."

Alexis frowns. "My kids don't eat hotdogs. Have you seen what's in those things?"

"Oh. Right. Of course. I'm also making burgers and brats, and I think Daddy has some chicken in the refrigerator. I'm sure we can find something for them to eat if you'll stay."

Alexis's gaze lands on all of us before it returns to her sister. "I don't know."

"Please." Scarlett rests a hand on her sister's forearm. "It would mean a lot to me if you'd stay. I haven't gotten to see the kids in a long time, and I'd really like to spend some time with them."

I'm about to tell Alexis to swallow her fucking pride when she finally relents. "Fine, we'll stay. Jason got called in to work today, so it's just the kids and me."

"Yay!" Scarlett squeals and throws her arms around her sister. Alexis, however, doesn't return the sentiment. Her arms hang limply at her sides.

"Is it just me, or does Alexis look constipated?" Dean murmurs, softly enough for only me to hear.

I punch him in the arm, and he laughs. "What? She does," he whispers. "That woman needs a beer and a good, hard fuck."

"Dinner was great, sweetheart." Rick tosses his napkin on the table and rubs his belly.

"Thanks, Daddy." Scarlett grabs his plate and kisses the top of his head. After putting his plate in the sink, she turns to grab mine, but I shake my head and stand up.

"No, ma'am. You cooked. You're not cleaning up after me."

"The dishes can wait," Rick declares. "It's too nice outside to spend the evening indoors. Let's take this to the deck. Chloe, I'll take you in a game of rummy."

"You're on, old man," she says.

"You don't have to tell me twice." Dean pushes away from the table and deposits his plate in the sink. "Rick, do you have any beer?"

"There's probably a few in the refrigerator. Grab me one, too."

"Daddy, I don't think that's a good idea," Alexis says.

Rick cuts a hand through the air. "One beer isn't going to kill me."

Chloe, Rick, and Dean move outside to the deck. Scarlett's niece and nephew go to follow, but she stops them.

"Wait. I have something for you two," Scarlett says, ignoring Alexis when she rolls her eyes.

Scarlett disappears and returns a minute later with two perfectly wrapped gifts. She hands one to Lucy and one to Declan.

"You didn't have to get them anything," Alexis says, crossing her arms over her chest.

Scarlett doesn't look at her sister when she responds, she's too focused on the kids, who are plowing through the shiny wrapping paper. "I know I didn't. I don't see them very often, and since I wasn't invited to their birthday parties, I thought I'd pick them up a little something."

She wasn't invited to their birthday parties? I knew things were rough between the sisters, but I didn't realize it was that bad.

"You sent them each a thousand dollars on their birthday."

"That was for their piggy bank. Today, they get their gifts."

"Cool!" Declan yells, holding up a white box with a picture of an iPad on the front.

"Yes! This is so awesome," Lucy says. "My very own iPad. I asked for one last Christmas, and Mom told me no."

"Thank you, Aunt Scarlett," they both say, wrapping their aunt in a hug.

"You're so welcome. The iPads are already set up and loaded with lots of games and age-appropriate books, and there's a five-hundred-dollar credit on each tablet so you can buy some more fun games and things."

"You're the best." Lucy hugs her one more time and then nudges Declan. "Come on, let's go show Grandpa."

The smile on Scarlett's face is priceless as she watches them bounce out of the house. Her love for those kids is endless, and anyone can see it. Except maybe Alexis, who looks like she wants to throttle her sister.

"Are you trying to make me look bad?" Alexis says.

"No." Scarlett shakes her head, her beautiful smile falling into a frown. "I'm trying to buy them a gift. I never get to see them."

"Oh, that's right, you just *buy* everyone's love."

"Alexis," I warn.

Scarlett looks at me with glossy eyes. "Will you give me a minute alone with my sister?"

Is she fucking crazy? I don't trust Alexis as far as I can throw her. I'm about to tell her just that when Scarlett says, "Please."

"Fine." I kiss her softly, a reminder that I'm here if she needs me, and I have her back, and then I give Alexis a pointed look and step out of the room. I don't go far because I want to be here in case Alexis turns into an even bigger bitch.

I hover in the hall, close enough to catch every word.

"I always let you walk all over me, and I'm done. God, Alexis, I can't do anything right with you. Everything I say and do is wrong," Scarlett says.

"I—"

"Would you just shut up for one minute and let me talk?" Scarlett says, interrupting Alexis.

Damn, it turns me on when she stands up for herself. I adjust my crotch. *Down, boy.*

"I don't know how to make you happy. You get pissy because I don't see the kids enough, but when I try to spend time with them, you don't let me."

"They're too young for you to fly them out to one of your shows."

"Maybe, but you didn't even send me an invitation to their birthday parties."

There's a long pause, followed by a sigh.

"You were on tour. I didn't think you'd come," Alexis says.

"You also didn't think I'd come home to take care of Daddy, but here I am. I would've found a way. I love Lucy and Declan, and I want to be here for stuff like that. I want to know when they get an *A* on a test or score a home run during one of their games. You shut me out at every turn, and I don't know what to do anymore."

"I'm sorry I didn't send you an invitation."

I have to hold onto the wall to keep from falling over. I bet it hurt Alexis down to her core to give that apology.

"Thank you," Scarlett says softly.

Lexi clears her throat. "And for what it's worth, not everything you do is wrong. It's not your fault that Daddy fell. It would have happened whether you were here or not. It's those damn rugs he insists on having. But please don't leave him by himself again."

"I won't. Trust me, I've learned my lesson. Now, about the kids—"

"Maybe we can set up FaceTime on their new tablets, and they can call you once a week."

"I'd really like that."

"As for everything else, let's just take it one day at a time. That's all I can give you right now."

"I can live with that."

I hear footsteps followed by the backdoor opening and shutting.

"You can come out now," Scarlett says, giving me the eye when I walk into the kitchen.

"What? I wasn't about to leave you in a room alone with your sister, especially with the way she's been acting lately."

"Thank you." She leans into me and rests her head on my shoulder. "She exhausts me. I don't know that I'll ever be able to please her, Tuck."

"It's not your job to please her. Alexis is responsible for her own happiness, not you."

"You're right, but it still hurts. I love my sister, and I want us to be close. I think a part of me always hoped that we would eventually get there, ya know? But I don't see that happening."

"For whatever reason, Alexis is holding onto a lot of resentment, and until she lets that go, I don't see it happening either."

"That doesn't make me feel better."

"Sorry, sweetheart." I kiss her nose. "Just being honest."

She sighs. "What do I do? Should I try talking to her?"

"I don't think so." I push a strand of hair out of her face. "I think you should wait for her to open up to you."

"What if she doesn't?"

"She will."

"But what if she doesn't?"

"Baby, you could what-if this to death. This is Alexis's problem, not yours. She's still adjusting to you being home. Give her time. Your sister might be a complete bitch, but she does have a heart."

"Are you sure about that?" Scarlett smiles at her snide remark and then covers her mouth. "I shouldn't have said that."

"You can say anything in front of me. I'm your safe place. Always. Now, enough about your sister, let's talk about us."

"My favorite subject."

"Good answer." I reward her with a kiss. "What are you doing this weekend? Chloe is staying with my mom on Friday night, and I'd love to take you out."

Scarlett frowns. "I wish I could, but I have to fly to L.A. for the weekend. Didn't I tell you about that?"

"No." I shake my head and tighten my arms around her.

"Sorry, I must've forgotten to mention it. Things have just been so crazy. There's a movie premiere. One of my songs is on the soundtrack, and I agreed to attend the premiere months ago. But I won't be gone long. I'll fly out Friday, and I'll be back by Sunday afternoon."

I hate that she's leaving. I hate it even more that I won't be with her, but I have to remember that this is part of her life. It's her job, and she does stuff like this all of the time.

"Who is going to stay with Rick?"

"My aunt, Clarice, offered to stay the weekend."

"That's nice of her."

"Yeah. Dad will enjoy having a new face around for a few days."

"I'll probably still pop in and check on him a few times."

Scarlett smiles up at me. "I figured you would. Thank you for looking after him."

"Your dad is like family to Chloe and me."

"I know he is. And he feels the same way about you two."

Scarlett kisses me, this time pushing it a little deeper. When she pulls back, I groan and rest my forehead against hers.

"This is going to be the longest weekend of my life."

She giggles. Music to my ears. "It'll fly by."

"I highly doubt that."

"You'll see. I'll be home before you know it."

"Dad!"

I'm in the kitchen, tidying up from dinner. Scarlett's only been gone for roughly twenty-four hours, and I'm already going out of my mind. I hate that she's not just a few yards away where I can see her or talk to her or hold her whenever I want. She belongs here, in New Hope, not across the country.

And I'm a dick for feeling this way. I know it. She's just doing her damn job, the same way I do when I put on the uniform every day and get into my squad car.

I have to share Scarlett with about forty million of her fans.

I've just never been very good at sharing.

And I'm taking my frustrations out on an innocent skillet, scrubbing it to within an inch of its life.

"Dad, did you hear me?"

"What's up, Chlo?"

"You have to see this! Scarlett's on the red carpet!"

I reach for a towel to dry my hands and hurry into the living room, where Chloe's watching some entertainment show.

And sure enough, there's my girl. Scarlett is dressed in a form-fitting red dress that stops about mid-thigh. Her legs are bare, and she's in a pair of red shoes that I can easily picture dangling from her feet as her calves are propped on my shoulders.

Down, boy.

"Oh, she's so pretty! That dress is just…wow. There's no way you'd ever let me wear something like that. Who's the guy she's with?" Chloe asks with a frown, and for the first time since I walked into the room, my gaze shifts from the woman I'm in love with to the man she's draped around. "Wait. That's Chase Walker. Holy crap, he's *amazing*, Dad! I have all of his songs on my iPad. And he's *hot*. Like, beyond hot. The way he dances is just dreamy. Do you think she could get me an autograph?"

"First of all, you're too young to look at men like that." She rolls her eyes, but I keep talking. "And second, shush."

My eyes narrow. They're both being interviewed, but I can't hear the questions over the roaring in my ears. Scarlett, *my* Scarlett, is sidled up next to this idiot, leaning into him as if they're more than just friends, while she smiles at the interviewer.

Do I have things wrong? Is she just fucking around with me while she's here in town, just something to keep her occupied until she goes back to her real life and this Chase dude?

My immediate reaction is *hell no.* We mean way too much to each other for that shit.

But my eyes can't deny what's right in front of me.

I shake my head and turn back to the kitchen.

"Dad, don't you want to watch this?"

"No," I reply, my voice flat. "I don't have any interest at all in watching that."

I feel like a chump. Of course, Scarlett freaking Kincaid isn't interested in anything long-term with me. I mean, look at her life.

She's all premieres and award shows. Tours and studio recordings.

She lives in Nashville, Tennessee. Not New Hope, South Carolina.

She's here to take care of her dad. End of story.

And it's best for everyone if I remember that.

14

~SCARLETT~

"YOU'VE GAINED TEN POUNDS."

I frown at Maureen in the mirror. She's the only person I know who can have ten pins pursed in her lips and still speak clearly.

"I've been taking care of my dad for a few weeks, Mo. I always gain a couple after I come off tour."

"This is more than a couple." She gives me the stink-eye, and I can't help but laugh. "You think it's funny, but it makes my job a shitshow."

"You're the best. And you know my body better than anyone. You've got this."

"Humph."

She scowls as she works on the side of the dress that Valentino sent over for tonight's premiere. Mo's been with me since my very first tour. At first, she just handled all of my onstage costumes, but as time passed, I asked for her to be my seamstress not only on the road but also for all of my events.

Like I said, Mo knows my body, and even with a few extra pounds, she'll make me look amazing.

"We told Valentino you were a size four," she insists.

"So, what am I now? A six?"

"Listen here, sassy pants, a six is way different than a four.

You're lucky they included some extra give in the seams so I can let it out where it needs it."

"Like I said, you've got this."

She rolls her eyes, and I gasp when she gets a little too close with the pins.

"Hey!"

"Serves you right."

Mo's in her late fifties. Her gray hair is long and frizzy, her face clean of makeup, and her voice is rough from too many years smoking cigarettes. I've never seen her without a tape measure around her neck.

She's one of my favorite people in the world.

"You love me."

"Humph," she says again, but I see the way her mouth tips up at the corners.

She totally loves me.

"I love the hemline on this one," I continue. It's scalloped and hits me at mid-thigh. All of the leg work I do has paid off in spades. I have the best legs in country music, and I'm damn proud of it. "Once I get those heels on, my legs will look amazing."

"What's our timeline?" Mo asks.

"We've got a couple of hours."

"Good. You can take it off, and I'll work my magic. For God's sake, eat a salad."

"Love you, too, Mo."

She mumbles to herself as she stomps out of the room, and I laugh again. Mo's always a little grumpy. It's part of her charm.

Once I'm out of the dress and into my robe, I'm ushered over to hair and makeup. By the time that's finished, Mo will be done with the dress, and I'll be ready to go.

I'd be happier if Tucker were here with me, but as much as I miss him and everyone else back home, I must admit, I'm having fun.

"Hey, gorgeous."

I look up in the mirror and grin at my friend, Chase.

"Hey, yourself."

"How's your dad?" he asks as he sits in the chair next to mine while the hair and makeup crew keep doing whatever it is they do.

"He's doing better. Getting therapy and stuff. But he's got a ways to go before he's back to his old self."

"Well, I'm glad to hear that he's going to be okay. I like Rick a lot."

"He likes you, too."

Dad's come to at least one show of every tour I've ever done, and back in the day, Chase and I toured a lot together, so Dad's met Chase a few times.

"What else's going on with you?" Chase asks.

"That's about it," I say, grinning.

He smiles and then shakes his head and laughs. "Who's the dude?"

"What dude?" I narrow my eyes and point to the hair and makeup crew, reminding him that ears are everywhere, and I don't need them to babble to the rags.

"I must have heard something somewhere," Chase says, but I know he'll want to talk more later. I'll tell him about Tucker in the limo.

"You'd better go put your monkey suit on."

"Fine." He sighs and stands, then leans over to kiss my cheek. "See you in a bit."

I sigh and close my eyes, determined to enjoy these few minutes of being pampered. Tonight will be busy. Loud. Lots of lights and noise.

The quiet is nice, even if it's brief.

"So, who is he?" Chase asks a few hours later in the back seat of the limo.

"Who's who?"

"The guy that finally stole Scarlett Kincaid's heart."

"Do I have hearts coming out of my head like in a cartoon or something?"

"Pretty much," he replies.

"Actually, I've been seeing someone I've known most of my life from back home."

"A civilian?"

"No ties to Nashville at all," I confirm.

"Wow."

"What?"

"That's brave of you, sugar."

"Listen. Relationships in the biz don't usually work well. Not everyone can be Faith and Tim."

"True."

"And I like him. A lot. He's a good guy. I think you'd like him, too."

"As long as he doesn't break your heart."

"If he does, I might get a hit single out of it."

That makes him laugh. The limo pulls up to the red carpet, and we both take a long, deep breath before the door opens, and pandemonium starts.

This movie is a huge blockbuster and is being covered by most of the media outlets. Thousands of fans line the barricades, hoping to catch a glimpse of their favorite actors from the film.

When Chase and I step from the car, the crowd erupts with screams and applause, and we immediately shift into publicity mode.

Smiles in place? Check.

Chase's arm wrapped around the small of my back, hand planted on my hip? Check.

My shoulder tucked against him? Check.

We walk down the carpet, and then stop on the mark and turn to the cameras, posing for what seems like an hour. Flashes erupt.

It's taken a decade to train my eyes to stay open wide, despite the onslaught of bright light.

Before long, we're ushered to where the entertainment channels have interviewers stationed to ask us questions.

"Scarlett! Chase!"

"Good evening," Chase says, and we spend the next thirty minutes answering the same questions over and over again.

Yes, I was honored to be asked to sing the title song for the movie. Of course, working with Chase is always wonderful. He's a good *friend*.

On and on we go until finally we make our way into the theater. The center of the place has been roped off for cast and crew. Once in our seats, we're treated to all the soda and popcorn a person can eat—all delivered to us, of course.

The dress may be gorgeous for the red carpet or for when I'm onstage, moving around, but sitting is a bit of a challenge.

"You don't look comfortable," Chase says.

"Yeah, well, I was pretty much sewed into this thing. Sitting cuts off my air supply."

He takes his jacket off and drapes it over my lap so I can get comfortable without putting on a show.

"Thanks."

Chase just winks and shoves some popcorn into his mouth.

I pull my phone out of my clutch. I've hardly spoken to Tucker since I got to L.A., so I shoot him off a text.

Wish you were here with me!

"Awe, that's so sweet," Chase says. I smack his shoulder but laugh.

"Mind your own damn business."

Tucker's reply is instant.

Looks like you're having enough fun without me. I'd just cramp your style.

I frown. What the hell is that supposed to mean?

You'd never cramp my style.

"Relationships are impossible for people like us," Chase says, shaking his head.

"Stop reading over my shoulder."

We'll talk when you get home.

"You told him you were coming with me, right?"

My lips part, and I shake my head. "No, I don't think so. I told him about the premiere, but that's it."

"There's your problem. Your boy is mad." Chase takes a drink of his soda and turns toward the movie screen when the lights dim.

"He is not."

What's there to be mad about? I'm only doing my job. Smiling for the camera with Chase is no different than Tucker pulling Maryanne Thompson's cat out of that tree.

I put the phone in my clutch, determined to enjoy the movie. I'm reading more into it than is really there. You can't tell what someone's tone is from a text anyway.

But why do I get the feeling that I'm in trouble?

I DIDN'T SLEEP last night. Which isn't good because I got on an early flight this morning from L.A. to Charleston, and then I had to drive down to New Hope.

It's mid-afternoon, and I'm just pulling into Dad's driveway, but I called Aunt Clarice ahead of time to give her the heads-up that I needed to have a conversation with Tucker before I came home.

She didn't even hesitate before she told me to take care of my business and come over when I'm ready.

Aunt Clarice always was my favorite.

I leave my bags in the car and hurry to Tucker's front door, hitting the doorbell extra hard as if that might make it ring louder inside.

"Scarlett!" Chloe exclaims as she opens the screen door and

launches herself into my arms. "You were gone forever. But you were *so pretty* in your dress."

"Thank you." I kiss her head as she leads me into the house and come to a stop when I see Tucker standing in the living room, his hands in his pockets, and no smile on his face.

"Hey, Chloe, why don't you go to your room while I talk with Scarlett?" Tucker says.

"I want to hear all about the movie—" she begins, but when she sees her father's face, his gaze which hasn't left *my* face, her shoulders slump, and she trudges up the stairs to her bedroom. Neither Tucker nor I say anything until we hear her door close.

"Hi," I begin.

"Hello."

This is *not* good. There's no hug. No kiss. No, *"I missed you so much, don't ever leave again."*

Nada.

"So, I get the feeling that you're pissed, and I'm probably dumped here, but I'll be damned if I can figure out why."

I cock a hip to the side and cross my arms over my chest. I'll be *damned* if I let him see me crumble. I'll cry later, when I'm alone.

"Chase Walker."

I tilt my head to the side. "My date?"

His eyes narrow.

"What about him?"

"Did you fuck him?"

"Did I—?" I shake my head, laugh humorlessly, and turn away from Tucker, heading to the front door. "You know what, Tuck? Go fuck yourself."

I make it onto the porch and to the top of the stairs when Tucker's hand wraps around my upper arm, and he spins me around to look at him.

"Scarlett—"

"No." My voice is even and low because we're outside, and at least a dozen ears can most likely hear us. "You don't *ever* have the right to speak to me like that. *You're* the one I'm currently fucking, as you so eloquently put it. But that's over, too."

"Listen to me, damn it."

I stop on the steps and shake my head, pissed as all get out that tears are threatening.

"I shouldn't have to explain myself to you."

"Well, it seems you do because I was minding my own business, missing the hell out of you, when my daughter alerted me to the fact that you were wrapped around that son of a bitch like white on rice."

I spin, my mouth gaping. "She did *not* say that."

"No, she didn't have to. I saw it."

I march past him back into the house where no one can hear us, relieved when I hear my own music blaring from upstairs in Chloe's room.

Once Tucker shuts the door, I round on him.

"So, you think that because I had a date to a function that was scheduled six months ago, I must be sleeping with said date?"

"Scar—"

"No, I want to make sure I understand what the hell is running through your pea-brained head, Tucker Andrews."

"I didn't like seeing you sidled up to the guy, okay? His arm was wrapped around you, his hand planted on your ass. You were as cozy as could be."

"His hand was on my *hip*, thank you very much, and we have to be cozy because that's what's expected, damn it. Chase has been my friend for *years*. He's just my friend. And we sang the damn song together, so we went to the premiere together."

"You failed to mention that when you told me you were leaving town."

"Would you like me to copy you in on my schedule?" I plant my hands on my hips. "Am I supposed to get permission every time I have to be somewhere with a man?"

"Cut me a break here, Scar," he says with a sigh and drags his hand down his face. "I'm not used to the celebrity lifestyle you live. I'm just a small-town cop."

"You're not *just* anything."

"And I've fallen in love with a woman who's larger than life. When I looked at that television screen and saw you standing there with him, I almost lost my shit. I *never* lose my shit, Scarlett. I didn't like it."

"You…you, what?"

"I didn't like it."

"Before that."

He frowns as if he doesn't know what I mean, but then his face clears, and he licks his lips. "I said that out loud, didn't I?"

"I think so."

He worries his lower lip between his teeth as he watches me from across the room.

"I felt like a damn fool."

"No." I shake my head slowly. "You're no fool, and I didn't say anything about Chase because I honestly didn't think anything of it. He was my date. Is my friend. But *you're* my lover, Tucker. You're the one I think about and miss when you're not around. You're the one I can't keep my hands off of."

I walk toward him, relieved when his hands come around my waist, and he pulls me close, staring down into my face.

"Now, what did you say?"

"I love you so much I ache with it," he whispers as if each word is painful to admit. "And I'm afraid you'll destroy me before all is said and done."

I launch myself up, confident that he'll catch me as I wrap myself around him and seal my lips to his, kissing him with everything I've got. When I pull back, I'm breathing hard, and I frame his handsome face in my hands and smile down at him.

"I love you, too, Tucker. And if anyone winds up with a broken heart, it'll be me. I hated that you wouldn't answer your phone last night."

"I'm an ass."

"Yeah, you are. No silent treatment, you hear me? Ever. Yell at me, whatever you have to do, but you *must* talk to me. Because there will be times that I can't be here, and you better answer your goddamn phone."

"Yes, ma'am," he says, the muscles in his jaw clenching. "I'm sorry."

"I'm sorry, too."

"But next time, give me a heads-up. At least let me know which asshole will have his hands all over you."

I grin. "Deal. But for the record, no one will have their hands all over me."

"What now?"

"Well, your daughter is upstairs, and I have to go take over for Aunt Clarice, so we can't get naked and have make-up sex."

"Rain check?" His lips twitch into a grin.

"Bet your sexy ass."

15

~ TUCKER ~

"STAY TOGETHER," I tell Chloe and her friend Jenny as they disappear into the crowd. Springfest is New Hope's annual music and art festival and always brings a ton of visitors.

People from all over mill about, laughing and dancing. Artists paint giant chalk murals on the roads, and various bands are scattered about, playing anything from country to jazz to rock.

For the first time in I don't know how long, I'm off work and looking forward to enjoying the festival with my two girls and Rick.

"I'm not sure they heard you."

I smile down at Scarlett and take her hand in mine. "You think?"

Scarlett chuckles and slows our pace so her dad can keep up. When she reaches for his elbow, he scoffs and swats her hand away.

"Stop fussing over me, I'm fine."

"Grandpa! Aunt Scarlett!"

We all turn at the sound of Lucy's and Declan's voices. They're running toward us at warp speed with Lexi and Jason not too far behind. Lucy launches herself into Scarlett's arms and goes on and on about some new game she downloaded onto her iPad.

Jason reaches out a hand for me to shake. "How's it going, Tucker?"

"Not too bad," I reply. "Yourself?"

"Well, I'm here and not at the hospital, so that's always a plus." We both laugh, and he turns a kind eye to Scarlett. "Hey, Scar. It's good to see you."

She untangles from her niece and pulls Jason in for a hug. "It's good to see you, too."

"Daddy, where is your walker?" Lexi chides, wrapping an arm around Rick's back as though she can actually keep him from falling.

"Don't need it."

Lexi's eyes widen. She looks from Rick to Scarlett. "What's he talking about?"

"The physical therapist says he's doing great, healing much faster than they anticipated. He's been moving around without his walker or cane for four days now."

"And no one thought to tell me?"

"Pull the stick out of your butt," Rick says, causing Declan and Lucy to snicker. "Can't you just be happy for me?"

Lexi's face softens. "Of course, I'm happy for you, but you're still my daddy, and I worry about you."

"How about you worry about getting me a lemon shake-up and a funnel cake?"

"Yeah!" Declan shouts, jumping into the air.

Scarlett laughs and ruffles Declan's hair. "Come on. Lemon shake-ups and funnel cakes for everyone. My treat."

"We'll get some tables," Lexi says, veering her family to the left while Scarlett and I go in search of the snacks.

"Hey, lovebirds." Scooter sidles up on the opposite side of Scarlett and puts an arm around her shoulders.

"Get your hands off my girl."

"What girl? This girl?" He looks at Scarlett and feigns shock. "Is she your girl? I didn't know, because no one tells me anything."

Scarlett loves the banter and the attention. "Hey, Scooter?" she says.

"Yes, darlin'."

"I'm Tucker's girl."

Damn, that sounds good.

"'Bout damn time." Scooter drops a kiss to her head and squeezes my shoulder. "Stop by the beer tent later, and we'll celebrate."

"Not tonight. I've got Chloe."

"And I've got dad," Scarlett adds.

Scooter stops in his tracks and blinks at us. "Is this how it's going to be from now on? What are you two, seventy?"

I shrug. "Sorry."

It's a halfhearted apology, mostly because I'm not sorry. There's really nothing I love more than being here with Scarlett and our families, enjoying the time together.

"Whatever." Scooter waves us off, walking backward through the crowd. "Just come into the bar sometime and have dinner. I miss your ugly mug."

"Will do."

We wave goodbye to Scooter and turn toward the food cart, only to be stopped by a little girl clutching a pad of paper in her hand and wearing a giant smile.

"Can I have your autograph?" The little girl thrusts the paper toward Scarlett, only to be pulled away by her mother.

"Ari, what did I tell you? You can't just go up and ask Miss Scarlett for her autograph. She's here spending time with her family. It's rude."

"It's okay. I don't mind." Scarlett takes the notepad and pen from the little girl.

"Are you sure?" the woman says, looking apologetic.

"Absolutely." Scarlett squats down in front of the little girl. "What's your name?"

"Arianna. My friends call me Ari. I'm a big, big fan of yours. I really wanna go to one of your concerts, but Mom says they're all too far away. Maybe someday if you have a concert here, she'll take me."

Scarlett's head snaps up. She looks at the girl with a furrowed brow. "I will mention it to my manager. I promise that my next tour will include somewhere close by, and if you write down your address for me, I'll send you three tickets."

"Really?" Ari's eyes light up. "That's so awesome. Thank you so much."

"You don't have to do that," the mom says, shaking her head when her daughter squeals in delight.

"I want to." Scarlett signs the top sheet of paper on the pad and hands it back to the little girl, who scribbles her address on another page. She tears it off and gives it to Scarlett.

"I don't need three tickets. I only need two. One for me, and one for my mom."

"I thought maybe you'd want to bring a friend," Scarlett suggests.

Once again, the girl screams, and I have to take a small step back before she blows my eardrums. Scarlett is completely unaffected. I guess she's gotten used to this over the years. She'll probably be deaf before we're fifty. I picture us in rocking chairs on the front porch forty years from now, and me having to scream to get her to hear me. I smile at the thought.

"Thank you so much." Ari bounces on her toes as though she's about to shoot off like a rocket. "Can I hug you?"

Scarlett answers the girl by wrapping her in a tight hug. When she lets go, Ari smiles, gives us one last wave, and walks away with her mother.

We're stopped once more on our way to the food vendor, by a group of girls begging for a selfie. Scarlett takes it all in stride, talking to the girls and smiling for the camera. She even signs a couple of shirts and records a short video for one of the girls' friends who is in the hospital recovering from surgery.

"Have fun!" Scarlett waves goodbye to the girls and tucks herself back under my arm.

"You're good with your fans," I tell her.

"They're good to me. If it wasn't for them, I wouldn't be doing what I love."

"I disagree. You're famous because you have an amazing voice. You're damn good at what you do."

"I appreciate the compliment, but it's more than that. I've met several people along the way who have voices better than mine, but they didn't make it anywhere. I got lucky. Right place, right time, loyal fans."

"Do you ever get tired of it?" I ask.

Scarlett and I haven't talked much about her career since she returned home, but it's a huge part of her life, which means I want to know more about it.

"Being famous?"

"All of it. Touring, performing night after night, award shows, premieres, interviews, fans. It has to get exhausting."

"It does, but when I start to get overwhelmed, I remind myself that this is all fleeting. One of these days, it'll slow way down or come to an end, and all I'll have left are the memories."

"And what happens when it comes to an end? What then?" I ask, stepping in at the end of the food cart line.

"I don't know. I haven't thought that far."

"Come on, surely you picture something. Marriage? Kids? A big house with a white picket fence and a golden retriever?"

"I honestly haven't thought about it. I've always just lived day to day." Scarlett props her chin on my chest and gazes up at me. "This is a pretty deep conversation for a music festival."

Okay, maybe I shot too far, too fast with the marriage and kids thing, but I'm genuinely curious as to where she sees herself. I was also a little hopeful that she'd say that wherever she is and whatever she's doing, she pictures Chloe and me right there with her.

"What about you?" she asks. "Where do you see yourself?"

With you. Maybe another kid—or two. But I can't tell her that. I can't put my dreams and my heart on the line when I don't know where she stands.

"Probably in prison for killing Chloe's first boyfriend."

Scarlett tips her head back and laughs as we move to the counter. All conversation about the future is set aside when the worker asks for our order.

"CAN I go home with Jenny? Please, please, please." Chloe lays it on thick, hugging me and blinking up at me with those big eyes of hers.

"Let her go," Rick says from his spot across the table. "She's only young once."

"You heard the man. Go," I concede, earning a wet kiss to the cheek from my daughter. "Wait, what about clothes and a toothbrush."

"She can wear some of my clothes, Mr. Andrews," Jenny says. "And we have an extra toothbrush she can use."

"Sounds like you girls have thought of everything." I look at Jenny's mom, who is standing behind the girls. "Are you sure you don't mind her going home with you?"

"Positive. I can drop her off in the morning on my way to work."

"I work tomorrow. I'll have to call Grandma and see if—"

"She can come hang with me," Scarlett says.

"Really?" Chloe throws her arms around Scarlett. "Thank you, Scarlett. I'd love to spend the day with you and Rick."

Scarlett pats Chloe's arm. "We have to get the okay from your dad first."

"I'm okay with it if you are."

Scarlett nods, and Chloe high-fives her friend. "Thanks, Dad. See you tomorrow, Scarlett."

We all wave goodbye, even Alexis, who doesn't seem as stiff as she was earlier when we came back with the food.

A band starts playing an old rock song, and Rick stands up. He taps Lucy on the shoulder. "I love this song. Let's go dance."

"Okay," Lucy giggles, getting up and taking her grandpa's hand.

"What about me?" Declan frowns.

"You can come, too."

Rick and the kids boogie their way onto the dance floor, and a second later, Jason excuses himself to talk to someone he knows.

Scarlett claps and smiles as she laughs at her dad. I notice Lexi watching her sister and, eventually, she slides down the bench and puts herself across from Scarlett.

"Hey."

Scarlett pulls her eyes from the dance floor and looks at Lexi. I hate that her smile falters. "Hey."

"So, Dad is really doing better?"

"Yeah. The physical therapist said that he's regained ninety percent of his strength and full use of his hand. Occupational therapy only has two more visits, and then they're done."

"I guess he won't be needing you anymore."

Oh, shit.

Scarlett's face hardens. "I guess not."

Alexis looks taken aback by the harsh tone of Scarlett's voice. "I—I didn't mean that in a bad way. I wasn't trying to be rude. I meant it very literally."

Scarlett doesn't look convinced, and after a long, awkward pause, Lexi clears her throat. "I'm sorry."

"It's okay. I shouldn't have jumped down your throat."

"I don't mean about what I just said," Lexi clarifies. "I mean for the way I've treated you since you arrived."

I clear my throat, and Lexi rolls her eyes.

"And also for the way I treated you before...over the last several years."

"I forgive you."

"Just like that? I've been a complete bitch. I'm probably still going to be unbearable at times."

Scarlett laughs, then reaches across the table and rests a hand on Lexi's. "We're sisters. Of course, I forgive you. I still think we need to have a serious talk about our issues with each other, but this is a good start."

Lexi takes a deep breath and blows it out. She looks as though the weight of the world has been lifted from her shoulders. "What now?"

"Now, I need to get Dad home before he breaks a hip on the dance floor."

"I meant in your life."

Scarlett reaches for my hand under the table. She's as surprised at Lexi's change in behavior as I am, but I know by the gentle squeeze she gives me that she's happy. And if my girl is content, then so am I.

"Well, I'll be here until Dad gets officially released"—she looks up, her eyes finding mine—"and then...I don't know what. I guess that's something I need to figure out."

"As much as I love seeing my girls smiling at each other, I'm ready to go home." Rick is panting and out of breath from his spin around the dance floor as he approaches the table. "This body can't move like it used to."

"Do you need me to go to the car and grab your walker?" I ask, standing up.

"Nah, I'm good. Just a little winded."

Scarlett stands up. We all say our goodbyes and make our way to the car. It's dark by the time we get back to Rick's house. He retreats to his room with a murmured "goodnight."

"Do you mind if I take a quick shower?" Scarlett asks. "I'd ask you to join me, but that's probably not very appropriate with my dad down the hall."

"You're killing me." I groan and pull her into my arms. I kiss her hard, showing her with my lips just how badly I want to be in the shower with her. When we break apart, I slap her ass. "Go, while I still have the strength to step away."

"I'll be quick."

With Chloe at a friend's house, there's no rush for me to leave, so I kick my shoes off by the door and sit on the couch. Rather than turn on the TV because I don't want it to be too loud for Rick if he's trying to go to sleep, I lean my head back and close my eyes.

I must doze off because I wake up sometime later with a warm woman in my lap, kissing her way up the side of my neck. She nibbles my ear, and my cock stirs to life.

"Wake up, sleepyhead," she breathes.

I blink my eyelids open. Scarlett is indeed sitting on my lap. She's wearing nothing but a towel and a smile. I slide my hands up her thigh and under the terrycloth. I'm met with soft, warm flesh, and her lips part when I drag a finger down her core.

"Baby, we can't do this here." My body disobeys my words when my hand slides to the small of her back and pulls her to me. Scarlett answers by grinding her bare pussy against my jeans. I'm hard as a rock and ready to pound into her, but this isn't exactly the place for that to happen.

"Daddy is asleep. I checked on him."

"You're a minx."

"I'm horny, and I want you inside of me." Scarlett releases her towel. It falls, exposing her breasts. Her nipples are puckered tight, begging for my mouth, and who am I not to give them what they want?

I lean forward and capture a tight bud in my mouth. I suck and lick and bite until Scarlett's writhing against me. With my hands on her waist, I guide her over my rigid cock, which is pushing uncomfortably against the seam and zipper of my jeans. Her body draws tight, her breaths coming in short little pants, and then I slip two fingers inside of her. Three strokes and she's falling apart in my arms. Her pussy spasms against my fingers, sucking them deep.

Her soft body collapses against mine, and when she catches her breath, she sits up. Her eyes are glazed over, her bottom lip plump from her biting on it. Without a word, she reaches for my jeans. I watch her pop the button, lower the zipper, and ease me out of my boxers.

Scarlett lifts onto her knees, positions my cock at her entrance, and slowly lowers herself on top of me.

What we're doing is damn risky with Rick asleep in the other room, but right now, I can't bring myself to care.

I start to move my hips, but Scarlett shakes her head and stills me with a hand to my chest. "It's my turn. Let me make you feel good."

I lean back against the couch. "You always make me feel good," I say, my hands roaming every inch of her delicious, naked body.

My beautiful girl moves on top of me, rotating her hips, lifting herself up and then dropping back down. Her hands are everywhere. I feel her start to tighten around me. She's close and, fuck, so am I.

There's nothing I want more than for us to fall over the edge together.

"Look at me," I command gently.

Scarlett blinks her eyes open. They bob heavily, but she manages to keep her eyes on mine.

"I love you." I push my hands into her hair, pull her down for an achingly sweet kiss, and breathe her in. "I love you so much."

Tears build in her soulful brown eyes. "I love you, too."

Four words are all it takes, and I'm spiraling out of control. My body stiffens beneath hers, and a zap of electricity works its way up my spine before scattering down my arms and legs. My balls tighten, and when I feel a moan working its way up my throat, I seal my lips to hers in an attempt to keep us both quiet.

Scarlett falls with me. Our bodies spasm and jerk against each other as we float down from our high. There aren't words for what just happened. It was love at its finest; two bodies coming together in the purest form. And when Scarlett tilts her head to the side and smiles at me, I know without a doubt that she's it.

This girl is my forever.

16

~ S C A R L E T T ~

"I'M SO impressed with your progress," Gretchen says to Dad just a few days later after a particularly grueling physical therapy session. "In my professional opinion, my work here is done."

"Really?" I ask, my voice full of hope and excitement.

"Really." Gretchen smiles at Dad and then gives him a big hug. "You've done a great job with your exercises, and frankly, you've recovered incredibly well. Keep up the good work. And if you ever have questions or concerns, I'm only a phone call away. As soon as I get back to the office, I'll let your doctor know that I'm releasing you."

"Thank you," Dad says, patting Gretchen's back. "I couldn't have done it without you."

"Oh, I know," Gretchen says with a sassy wink. "I'd better get going. Be sure to follow up with your doctor, and let me know if you need anything."

She waves before walking out of the house, and I wrap my arms around Dad's middle, holding on tightly, so relieved that he's going to be okay.

"I'm so proud of you," I say against his chest. He smells the same as he has since I was a little girl, of Old Spice. "You knocked it out of the park."

"Being an overachiever runs in the family," he says with a laugh. "It feels good to be pretty much back to normal. I'll keep a cane nearby for when I'm tired, but I'm feeling fantastic. In fact, you don't need to babysit me all the time anymore. I got rid of those damn rugs in the kitchen, and you heard Gretchen. I'm fine."

I frown and follow him into the kitchen where we each grab a bottle of water out of the fridge and then walk outside. Summer is quickly approaching, along with long, hot days. But today is pleasant with a cool breeze.

"You know I worry about you."

"And I appreciate it, honey. But maybe it's time for you to start thinking about going back to your normal routine."

I take a sip of water, thinking it over. I miss the music and my friends in Nashville. My routine.

But if I go back to what I know in Tennessee, I won't have Tucker.

And that just seems out of the question.

"You went and fell in love with him, didn't you?" Dad asks with a satisfied smile on his lips.

"I did," I admit softly, looking across the yards to Tucker's house. He should be getting home from work anytime. Chloe went to Jenny's house again. It seems the two girls have become inseparable. "And I'm stupid."

"I didn't raise a stupid girl."

I sigh and shift my gaze to my father. Lexi looks just like him, with her brown hair and blue eyes. I get my darker features from our mother. I wonder if looking at me for all these years has been bittersweet for my dad.

"A relationship with Tucker seems impossible," I say. "He's here, and my career takes me *everywhere*."

"You'll work it out," Dad says with confidence, and before I can ask him how he thinks that's possible, Tucker pulls up to his house. "Go see him."

"But you're—"

"Cleared to go back to normal activity," he reminds me with a proud grin. "Go see your guy. I'll get dinner started. We're having pork chops. Tell Tucker to join us."

And with that, Dad walks into the house.

I watch as Tucker steps out of his car and glances over at Dad's place. When he sees me sitting on the back porch, his face breaks out into a wide grin.

God, I'm going to miss seeing him every day.

I offer him a small wave, then walk across the grass to him, the same way I did when we were kids. Tucker sweeps me up in a hello kiss that would rival any chick flick out there.

"Hello there," I say when we come up for air.

"How was your day?"

"Pretty great. How was yours?"

"It's looking a lot better now." He laces his fingers with mine and leads me into his house. "Is Lexi with your dad?"

"No, Dad's by himself." Tucker turns and raises a brow. "He was just given the okay to go back to normal from Gretchen."

"That's the best news I've heard all day."

"Me, too." Tucker sits on the couch with a sigh, and I climb into his lap, lay my head on his chest, and soak him in. "Was work bad?"

"We had an accident," he says and buries his lips in my hair. "Two little ones didn't make it."

"I'm sorry." I kiss his chest. "I guess I forget about this side of your job. I always think about speeding tickets and drug cartels."

He chuckles and gives me a squeeze. "It's usually somewhere in the middle of those two."

"When was the last time you took a vacation?" I ask.

"A couple years ago," he replies. "Why?"

"Well, if you can swing it, I'd like to go to Nashville for the weekend. I haven't been home in months, and I'd like to check on my house and stuff. Honestly, I'd like to show you and Chloe what I've been up to all these years."

"When would you like to leave?"

"Friday morning."

"That's two days away."

"I know." I'm not looking at him. Honestly, I'm nervous that he'll turn me down. "But Chloe's last day of school is tomorrow, and you usually have weekends off."

"I'll make it work," he says, and my head whips up in surprise.

"Really?"

"Sure. Getting out of town for a few days will be fun. Chloe might kill me if I say no."

"We wouldn't want that." I kiss his cheek. "I'll make sure Lexi can look in on Dad. I know he's been given the all-clear, but looking in on him won't hurt."

"I guess I'd better make a couple of calls," Tucker says with a smile. "Seems my lady wants to take a trip."

"Seems she does," I confirm. "So, I'll go and let you get things straightened out. Oh, and Dad said to tell you we're having pork chops for dinner."

"I'll be over in a few."

I lean in and kiss his lips softly before I pull away and saunter toward the door, more excited than I expected for the upcoming weekend away.

"See you soon."

"THIS IS MY BEDROOM?" Chloe asks, looking around the guest suite on the second floor of my home in Nashville. We just arrived at the house, and I'm pleased to see that my staff aired out all the rooms, changed the linens, and stocked the kitchen for us.

"Don't you like it?" I also look around the space, taking in the big, four-poster bed and the white linens. "You have your own bathroom in here, and a balcony in case you want to get some fresh air."

"Oh my gosh, it's *awesome,*" she says, her voice shrill. "It's a princess's room. I could have twenty people over for a sleepover."

"Oh, good. You scared me." I kiss her head and look over to Tucker, who's leaning against the doorframe, his hands in his jeans' pockets, watching us. "You can unpack your things if you like and get comfortable. Your dad and I will be downstairs."

"Okay. Dad, can I have my phone so I can FaceTime Jenny and show her this room? She won't believe it."

"Sure," Tucker says, passing her the iPhone.

"Thanks," Chloe says. "And thanks for this cool room, Scarlett."

"My pleasure." I pat her shoulder, and then Tucker and I walk down the hall to the other side of the house where the master bedroom is. "Should you also stay in a guest room? Of course, I *want* you with me, but Chloe's so young, and I don't want to assume—"

"Chloe and I talked about this," he says, surprising me. I walk into my bedroom, and Tucker joins me. The staff has already brought up our luggage. "She's cool with me staying in here with you as long as I don't tell her about the kissing."

I feel my lips twitch into a grin. "Well, I think we can manage that."

"Your home is beautiful." His voice is soft, but I feel him holding back.

"But?"

"But it's a little intimidating. I don't think I've ever been in a house this big."

I nod thoughtfully. "I get it. It's a big house. But there's also a recording studio you haven't seen, along with a gym and a pool."

"Well, Chloe will love that."

"Do *you* love it?"

He walks to the double doors that open out to the balcony that overlooks the pool and gardens. We step out and lean on the cement railing.

"It's fun," he says at last. "Different."

"It's not as intimidating as you think," I assure him. "The staff doesn't stay all the time. They meet me here after I've been gone for a long time to help me get settled. But then they're gone. Trust me, I don't keep a butler and a maid every day."

"I didn't say anything about that."

"I saw your wheels turning." I take his hand in mine because the distance is killing me. "The maid comes once a week. I also have a gardener and a pool boy."

"Of course, you do."

"I mean, I have a pool," I remind him. "Hence, the pool boy."

He laughs and reaches up to tuck a piece of hair behind my ear. "It's great, Scar. You've done really well for yourself. Thanks for having us."

"Let's take the weekend to relax," I suggest. "We can go into the city if you want to do the tourist thing. We can swim, or veg, or whatever. No agenda."

"Sounds good." He leans down to kiss me, but we suddenly hear gagging noises behind us.

"Seriously," Chloe says. "Ew. There is a child present."

"You weren't present four seconds ago," Tucker says, ruffling her hair and earning a scowl. "Haven't you ever heard of knocking? Did your father raise you in a barn?"

"The door was open," Chloe reminds him and rolls her eyes. "And my father is the one born in a barn."

I love watching them banter. They're funny, comfortable with each other, and you can see the love between them.

Tucker is an excellent dad.

It's just another reason for me to love him more than anything in the world.

"Is that a pool?" Chloe asks with excitement, leaning over the railing. "Oh my gosh, we gotta swim! I brought my suit, just in case. I think I read in *People* magazine a few years ago that you had a pool. Dad, we need a pool! I'm gonna go change. Last one in's a rotten egg."

She runs through the bedroom and toward her room, leaving us grinning after her.

"So, I guess first up is swimming," I say with a laugh.

"How can you resist that?" he agrees. "And the last one in's a rotten egg, so let's go."

THE WEEKEND FLEW by in a flurry of activity. We ate, relaxed, laughed, and swam. It's been wonderful. I don't want it to end.

"How is it Sunday evening already?" The night is quiet around us. We're sitting out on the master balcony on plush furniture, with chips and *queso* as a snack because I got hungry. "Time sure flies when you're being lazy."

"We haven't been lazy," Tucker protests with a full mouth. "We've been swimming and recording awful songs in your studio for two days."

"There's that," I agree with a grin. Chloe *loved* the studio, and we spent all morning today laying down tracks. "With some voice lessons, she might—"

"Still be tone deaf," Tucker finishes for me. "She's my daughter, and I think she's the most brilliant child on the planet, but even I can admit that she has no future in singing."

I'm laughing, holding my sides. "She's not that bad."

Tucker pops another chip into his mouth and stares at me. "Really?"

"Okay, she's pretty bad. But she's great with the guitar."

"That I'll agree with," he says. "She practices all the time."

"It shows. We barely left the house since you arrived." That's an understatement. We've only been to the grocery store three miles up the road to stock up on more food. "We didn't go to the Opry, or any of the amazing restaurants, or anything."

"We didn't mind."

"Chloe seems to enjoy it here." God, I'm nervous. Why am I so damn nervous? Oh, yeah, because my very happiness might depend on how this conversation goes. No pressure or anything.

"She loves it," he agrees, scraping the last of the *queso* out of the bowl. "She might have grown gills this weekend, with as much as she was in the pool."

"She loves to swim." I look out over the pool area in question and take a deep breath. "Do you think this is somewhere you might be able to see yourself living?"

I bite my lip and watch as a frown forms between Tucker's eyes. He sets the bowl down, swallows the food in his mouth, and licks his lips.

"I mean, not right away, of course. I know it takes time, and maybe I'm jumping the gun a bit."

"No."

I blink rapidly. "No?"

He clears his throat and shakes his head. "I couldn't live here."

"Couldn't, or wouldn't?"

"Both. We can't move to Nashville, Scar. My job, Chloe's school, our *family* is in New Hope."

"Right." I nod, still blinking, but now trying to keep tears at bay. "Of course. Besides, we've never really said this thing between us is going anywhere."

"Stop talking," he says with frustration. "I'm not telling you that we aren't going to be together, or that I'm not thinking about the long-term with you. Do you think I throw the *L* word around to everyone?"

"No, I—"

"But it's not as easy as Chloe and I just packing up the house and relocating. It's not that simple."

"I understand that." I nervously pluck at a loose thread on my chair. "I do. It's just…I'm based out of here. I have dozens of people who rely on me, and my career isn't something I can just pick up and move."

"I understand that, too, and I would never ask you to give it up."

"So, it's impossible," I whisper. "I shouldn't have brought you here."

"Hey, the Scarlett I know isn't this dramatic."

I stare at him in horror. "Are you fucking kidding me? We basically just decided that our relationship won't work, and you're calling me *dramatic*?"

"Who said our relationship won't work? I didn't say that."

"Oh, for the love of Moses." I stand and walk into my bedroom. "I'm done discussing this."

"You brought it up."

"And I'm dropping it," I reply coldly. "Because the alternative to you moving here is us being fuck-buddies on the rare occasion I get to New Hope, and I'm not going to insult either of us by insinuating that that's what you meant."

"Now you're just pissing me off."

"Thanks for catching up to the conversation at hand." I plant my hands on my hips and frown at him. "And thanks for being so willing to compromise. It's the foundation of a functional relationship, after all."

"Scar, everything Chloe and I know is in South Carolina. She's in school there, with friends and a whole community that loves her."

"Nashville has schools," I inform him. "And it's not like I'm suggesting we never go back to New Hope again. I know I don't get home often—"

"Or ever."

"I'll buy a private plane for God's sake, and we can fly over any time."

"I don't have a solution," he says, holding his hands out to his sides. "I know that I don't want to lose you. And I also know that Nashville isn't the answer for me."

"So, I'm the only one who should bend here because I'm not a mother, and I have money." I nod, feeling hurt all the way to my soul. "I guess it's good to know now what your expectations are."

"I don't have any fucking expectations," he growls.

153

"Well, I do. I expect you to consider the whole picture and come into a conversation with an open mind."

"I'm not the only one unwilling to bend. You just said your life is here and you can't pick up and move. Why aren't you compromising, Scarlett?"

"There is nothing productive about this conversation."

"Agreed."

I'm breathing hard with anger and disappointment. Sadness. Frustration. "The other guest suite is down the hall."

"You're kicking me out because you didn't get the answer you wanted?"

"I'm kicking you out because I'm mad at you."

Tucker shakes his head and blows out a breath. "I guess you'll know where to find me then."

He turns on his heel and stalks out the door, closing it firmly behind him.

I've ruined everything. I just had to share my home with Tucker and Chloe. I wanted them to see where I live.

I wanted them to just shift right into place, into my life, without any hiccups.

"I'm an idiot," I mutter and turn to the bathroom. I need a hot shower, and I need to let go of some of this angry energy.

17

~ TUCKER ~

"DAMN IT." I grab the pillow and flip to my side. When I can't get comfortable, I flop onto my back and stare up at the ceiling.

I've been tossing and turning for nearly three hours. It's well after midnight, and I should've spent the night making love to Scarlett, but here I am, brooding over our fight.

Normally, I'd be quick to concede because I don't like to fight, and I sure as hell don't want the woman I'm in love with mad at me, but I don't feel like I'm wrong in this situation. Scarlett wants me to bend, but she isn't willing to give me the same courtesy. And, okay, maybe I was a little harsh and quick to shut her down, but we've only been together for a short time. She left me once already, and who's to say she won't do it again? And how awful would it be for that to happen after I've shifted around my entire life to accommodate hers?

It would be fucking horrible.

I've given her my heart, but that doesn't mean I fully trust her with it.

But what's the alternative? Living a life without Scarlett? That's not something I want to even consider. Over the last several weeks, she's grown to mean so much to me. Our childhood friendship compounded into a love that I never thought I could feel for another human being. Aside from Chloe, of course.

If you love her that much, then why are you in this big-ass bed alone?

As much as I don't want to crawl back to her with my tail between my legs, I'm also not willing to leave things the way they are. We've come too far to let one little argument ruin what we've built.

I fling the covers off and stand up. I pull on a pair of sweats and open the door only to crash into a soft, warm body.

My hands reach out, and I grab her arms, slowing my momentum in an attempt to keep us from falling over. "Scarlett? Sorry, baby, I didn't mean to plow you over."

"That's okay," she says softly. "Where were you going in such a hurry?"

I drag my fingers through my hair. "I was coming to you."

"You were?" She sounds hopeful, and I hate that I can't see her expression.

I pull Scarlett into my room and flick on the bedside lamp, illuminating her beautiful face. Her eyes are glossy, and her cheeks are red, and I'll be damned if that doesn't make me feel like even more of an ass.

"Have you been crying?"

She shrugs and pulls her bottom lip between her teeth. "I don't like fighting with you. When you walked away, everything felt so final and..." Her words trail off, and she shakes her head as though she doesn't know what else to say.

"Damn, sweetheart, you could bring a man to his knees." I pull her into my arms and press my lips to the side of her head. "Scarlett, we are going to fight. There are going to be times when we need to take a step back and catch our breath, but we will never be over. I love you, and there's no way in hell I will let an argument like that come between us."

"I was coming for you."

"Huh?" I say, pushing a chunk of hair behind her ear.

"That's why I was standing outside your door. I couldn't take it anymore. After having you in my bed for the last few nights, I couldn't stand being in there alone. It just felt wrong, and I didn't know where we stood, and I hated that. I love you, Tuck, and I'm sorry I bombarded you with all of that."

"Don't be sorry. You said what was on your mind, and that's something I've always loved about you. You're honest to a fault, and there's nothing wrong with that. And I'm sorry, too."

"So, where do we go from here?"

I lay back on the bed and pull her down beside me. She curls into my side and rests her head on my chest. "I don't know about you, but I'm not ready to give this up. When I tell you I love you, I mean it. You're in my heart, and I have no plans of that changing. Ever."

"I feel the same way. But how are we going to make this work? If neither of us is willing to compromise, how do we move forward?"

"We make a choice to stay together," I say, skimming my fingers up and down her arm. "We make a choice to work it out. That doesn't mean we have to have all the answers right now. As our relationship grows, those things will become clearer. But for now, I think we simply make the choice to stick it out."

Scarlett props her chin on my chest so she can look at me. "You're right. We've known each other forever, but our romantic relationship is still new. Why push it?"

"Exactly. Right now, I can't commit to uprooting my life, and I know that your career will take you away from me, so we'll work on things one day and one situation at a time."

"Okay," she says, sounding pleased. "But one of these days, we'll have to revisit the topic, because we can't live like that forever."

"When that time comes, we'll sit down and have an adult conversation about how to move our relationship forward. Until then, we keep enjoying each other and let things progress naturally."

Her eyes twinkle. "And we keep having sex. Because the sex is great."

In less than a second, I have Scarlett pinned beneath me. "Of course, there will be sex. We might suck at compromising, but we're really good at sex."

"You mean more to me than that," she whispers, pulling her hands down my back.

"I know." I kiss her softly—once, twice, and a third time. "I hated being in this room without you tonight."

"Me, too. My bed was cold, and it felt empty. It was awful."

"Let's never do that again, okay? From now on, we work our shit out before it gets that far."

"Deal."

"And while we're on the subject of beds, I want you in mine."

"I am in yours." Scarlett rubs her soft body against mine. "Well, technically, it's my bed, but I gave it to you for the night."

"What I meant is that I want you in my bed for the remainder of your time in New Hope."

Scarlett blinks, her lips forming the perfect little O. "I just assumed that I'd stay with my dad until it was time to leave."

"And you can, if that's what you want to do, but I'd really like you with me. You said that Rick was cleared, and he's been by himself all weekend and has done fine."

Finally, Scarlett smiles. "You're right. And I'll still be super close in case he needs me."

"So, you'll stay with me?"

Scarlett pushes her fingers into my hair, palms the back of my head, and pulls me to her. "Yes, I'll stay with you."

"Can I please have a dog for my birthday?" Chloe curls her hands under her chin and begs me with her big, brown eyes. "Please, please, please."

"Chloe, you know we can't have a dog."

"But I'll have all summer to work on potty-training, and I'll teach it to learn different commands. I promise I'll take care of it all by myself."

"That's not why I'm saying no. We just don't have time. Maybe one of these days, but not right now."

Chloe gives me the stink-eye and sulks out of the room.

"When is Chloe's birthday?" Scarlett says, walking into the living room from the kitchen.

"In two weeks."

"I had no idea! Why didn't you tell me her birthday is coming up?"

"We've been so busy, and I never thought about it."

Scarlett rubs her hands together and gets a twinkle in her eye. "So, what are we getting her?"

"We?" I pull her onto my lap and press my lips to her ear. "I like the sound of that. And we are getting her a dog," I whisper.

"What?" Scarlett pulls back, a giant grin on her face. "But you just said—"

"I know what I said," I say, pressing a finger to my lips so she'll keep quiet. Chloe has been asking for a dog for years, but the timing has never been right. I think we're finally ready to make the commitment now that she's old enough to take on the responsibility. "It's going to be a surprise. The local shelter has some puppies that will be ready for their forever home by the time her birthday rolls around."

"Are you going to give it to her at her birthday party?"

"I don't know. I haven't thought about it yet."

"What're you doing for her party? What's the theme?"

"Theme?" I shake my head. "There is no theme. My parents, Dean, and Scooter will come over for a BBQ. Rick usually finds his way over, too. And you…I'm hoping you'll be here this year."

Scarlett nods and wraps her arms around my neck. "Of course, I'll be here. I don't have to go back for another month. But, Tucker, come on, she's turning twelve. You have to throw her a party."

"No, I don't. Chloe has never really had a big birthday party with friends."

Scarlett looks appalled. "That's all the more reason to throw her one now."

"I don't know." I scratch my head and think about it. "I'm a little short on time. Maybe next year."

"There's plenty of time! Let me plan it."

"I can't ask you to do that."

"You're not asking, I'm offering. I love Chloe, and I would love nothing more than to throw her a party she won't forget. Plus, I have mad party-planning skills."

How do I tell Scarlett no? She looks so darn excited, and it makes me happy that she wants to do this for Chloe. "Fine, but we have to agree on a price limit."

"There is no price limit."

"Scarlett, I'm not loaded."

"You're not, but I am. And before you even say it, you are not paying for a penny of this party. Consider it my gift to her," she says, ending her rant with a heated kiss to my lips.

Whatever rebuttal I was building up in my head dissipates when she slides her tongue into my mouth.

"Okay, this is really starting to get old," Chloe says.

Scarlett's cheeks turn a deep pink as she slides off my lap.

Chloe just shakes her head and walks out of the room.

"I'm going to get started on the planning," Scarlett whispers.

I barely see her for the next three days. She's on the phone, traveling from venue to venue, all the while keeping things very tight-lipped. When she said she was a mad party planner, she wasn't joking.

Finally, at the end of the week, after a long shift at work, Scarlett pulls me into the bedroom and hands me a file folder.

"What's this?"

"It's all the information on Chloe's party. Everything is detailed down to the napkins."

"Napkins? She isn't getting married, Scarlett."

Scarlett rolls her eyes. "Don't worry, they're paper napkins.

But they're super cute and match the rose gold color scheme perfectly. Go ahead, open it, let me know what you think."

I take a breath and open the file folder as I sit on the edge of the bed. Scarlett paces the length of my room as my eyes scan the pages, reading about everything from invitations, to a catered meal full of every kid's favorite foods, to party favors, and of course, napkins. She even hired a DJ. After reading every last word, I set the folder aside and pull Scarlett between my legs.

With my hands cupped to the back of her thighs, I look up at her. "You rented out the local water complex."

"I know!" Scarlett squeals, dancing a little jig. "Chloe and everyone in her class will have three hours of private access to the pool, all three water slides, and the splash pad. And do you know what's even better than having a pool party?"

"Having it catered?" I say since Scarlett booked a caterer.

"Besides that. I hired a DJ. How cool is that? It's going to be amazing. I really think the kids will like it."

"Not like. Love. They'll love it. I don't even want to know how much this is costing you."

"Don't ask, and I won't tell."

I shake my head, but I can't keep from smiling. "I can't believe you hired a DJ."

"Don't worry, I've already put together the playlist for the entire party. There will be no songs that talk about sex, drugs, or alcohol, and absolutely no cuss words."

"You've thought of everything. I think the party might top the puppy I'm getting her."

"I highly doubt that."

"I don't know how to thank you."

She wags her brows and smiles. "I have a few things in mind that you could do to thank me."

One look at her hooded eyes and I know exactly what my little spitfire is thinking. I stand up, picking her up along the way, and then toss her onto the bed. Scarlett laughs as she bounces, and then settles against my pillows.

"Where's Chloe?" she asks, glancing at the clock. "Shouldn't she be home from school by now?"

"She had running club after school. I don't have to go pick her up for another forty-five minutes," I say, pushing Scarlett's skirt up over her hips. "God, you're beautiful."

I slide her panties off and bury my face between her legs. Scarlett's hips lift, and she grinds herself against my face as I kiss, lick, and suck her pussy. When I push two fingers deep inside of her, I glance up the length of her body and nearly come in my pants.

She's propped up on an elbow. At some point, she managed to work down the front of her dress and is rubbing her breast. She twists and pinches her nipples into tight peaks while watching me.

"Fuck, that's hot," I say against her wet flesh.

Having her watch me as I eat her out is the sexiest thing. Her lips part, her breath comes in short pants, and then her legs begin to quiver, and I know that she's close. She struggles to keep her eyes on mine, and when I suck on her swollen clit and roll my tongue around it, she loses the battle.

Scarlett doesn't hold back. Her lids fall closed as she buries her fingers in my hair, holding me against her core as she screams through her release. I suck her dry and continue fucking her with my tongue until her body stops shaking.

"Jesus, Tucker," she rasps as I lift my face from between her legs.

She's all mussed with her dress bunched around her hips, and her breasts red from being played with.

"You liked that?"

"I loved that." A beat passes. Her eyes clear and then soften. "I love you, so much."

I reach between my body and the bed, work my pants down, and free my cock. "You're about to love me a whole lot more."

I crawl up the bed, kissing every inch of her body along the way until I'm hovering above her.

"I don't think that's possible."

~SCARLETT~

"THIRTY-FIVE," Chloe announces with the cutest little shimmy dance I've ever seen.

"Only thirty-five?" Tucker asks his daughter and winks at me. "That's practically your entire fifth-grade class."

"Dad, I don't want anyone to feel left out. I mean, this is the birthday party of the century. *Everyone* is gonna want to come. I even invited Stacy Pruitt, and she's a b-word sometimes."

"Then why invite her?" I ask, brushing my fingers through her soft hair. I settle in next to her, braiding the silky strands.

"Because she'll feel bad if she's the only one who doesn't get invited." Chloe shrugs one shoulder and examines her list of guests. One of the things I love most about this little girl is her big heart. She's always thinking of others' feelings.

She's an amazing kid.

"Did you invite your grandma and papa?"

"Yep, and Rick, Uncle Dean, and Scooter, too."

"Scooter in a bathing suit?" I ask, trying to get the image out of my head as Tucker laughs.

"I think the adults will watch the kids swim," Tucker says, watching me thread Chloe's hair through my fingers.

"You can swim, too," Chloe informs him, and I grin, imagining Tucker in his swim trunks.

The man has a body built for board shorts.

"I'll watch you guys. I'll be the lifeguard," he says, just as my phone rings. I glance down and frown when I see my manager, Susan's name flash on the screen. "I'd better take this."

I tie off the braid and quickly walk out the back door to the deck. I haven't spoken to Susan since I came to New Hope a month ago. I hope everything is okay.

"Hey, Sue. What's up?"

"You never reply to your email," she accuses, and I can see the stern look on her face.

"I know. Sorry. What's going on?"

"I need to confirm with you that you'll be in New York on Thursday. We have rehearsal and sound checks, and Mo said you'll need some costume alterations."

I pull the phone from my ear, glance at it, then press it to my ear once again. "What the hell are you talking about? I'm in New Hope for another three weeks."

"Negative, Ghost Rider," she replies. "If you'd read your damn email, you'd know that we rescheduled the shows and interviews we had to cancel when your dad had his stroke. We couldn't be super picky on dates because it's not like we scheduled two years out. I literally emailed you this itinerary two weeks ago."

"Two weeks ago, my dad was still unable to care for himself."

"Sorry, kiddo, the show must go on, and it's going on this Friday night."

Chloe's party is Saturday.

Okay, I can do this.

"I guess I can cancel—" she begins, but I interrupt her.

"No. We won't cancel twice, it's my fault for not looking at my email. But, Susan, from now on, you *have* to call me. And I have to be back in New Hope on Saturday."

She's quiet for a long moment.

"What's going on with you, Scar?"

"I'm living my life," I reply honestly. "For the first time in a *long* time, I'm enjoying the people who love me for more than my celebrity, and it feels damn good. So, I'll come do the show, but I'm coming home on Saturday."

"Understood." She clears her throat. "I'll text you if anything else comes up. The plane will be in Charleston on Thursday at ten in the morning, ready to take you to New York."

"Thanks." I frown, feeling bad for snapping at Susan. "And I love you. I'm just frustrated. I hate email."

"I should have called." She sighs. "It's just been busy here in the office, getting these dates rescheduled, and getting the band and singers together. It's a lot of working parts."

"And I love you for working so hard. Thank you. See you Thursday."

"See you soon." She hangs up, and I let out a long, breathy sigh.

Damn it.

I walk back into the house and hear Tucker and Chloe laughing in the living room where I left them.

"What's so funny?"

Tuck's smile falls a bit when he sees me. "What's wrong?"

"Absolutely nothing."

He narrows his eyes. "Don't lie to me."

"Okay. What's wrong, is you're having a good time in here, and I'm feeling left out. What gives?"

"Dad's just funny," Chloe says with a giggle. "And Jenny's mom should be here soon to get me. She's taking us shopping to buy new bathing suits for the party."

"I could take you," I offer, but Chloe shakes her head.

"It's totally okay. Jenny and I have it under control. Besides, you're doing a ton."

"It's my pleasure."

A car horn beeps, and Chloe jumps up to run outside. First, she hugs her dad, who whispers something in her ear. She nods happily. Then, she hugs me around the waist and hurries out of the house, running down the sidewalk to Jenny's mom's car. We follow her out onto the porch.

All three of them wave, and then they pull away.

"So, what's really going on?"

I sigh, feeling my shoulders sag in disappointment.

"I have to be in New York on Thursday."

I turn to him, but rather than respond, he just takes my hand and leads me back inside.

"I thought we had three more weeks."

"So did I." I fill him in on what Susan said about rescheduling the last of the concert dates. "So, I'll be gone for a couple of days, but I'll be back on Saturday for the party."

"That seems like a tight fit," he says, shaking his head.

"I don't care. I'll make it happen. I'll fly to Charleston after the concert if I have to and pull an all-nighter traveling home."

"No." He shakes his head adamantly. "That's too dangerous. Get some sleep after the show and head down the following morning."

"I'll be here," I insist, holding his hand tightly. "Wild horses couldn't keep me away."

"I hope so," he says. "Chloe would be crushed if you missed it. It's her first *real* birthday party."

"I know. And I'm as excited as she is. It's going to be great."

"THAT'S EVERYTHING," I say as I slam the trunk on my car and turn to Tucker, who helped me pack. I went ahead and gathered up pretty much everything I brought with me in the beginning, aside from some personal toiletries that I left in his bathroom, and some panties I left in the drawer he gave me in his dresser.

The weather's only getting hotter as summer takes over in the south, so I'll return with more appropriate clothes.

I'll be in New York, for God's sake. I can take a couple of hours Friday to do some shopping.

"I'll see you in two days," I remind him as he pulls me in for a long, slow kiss.

"See that you do," he whispers. "My bed's going to be damn empty without you in it."

"Good." I smile as he pats my ass playfully. "That means you'll miss me."

"That goes without saying."

"I thought we'd have longer before real life took over again. Before the things we talked about in Nashville would be an issue."

"It was bound to happen sooner or later," he reminds me and tucks a strand of my hair behind my ear.

"I was rooting for later." I lean in and press my ear to his chest, holding on for just a minute more.

"Hey, it's going to be okay." His big hands move over my back in soothing circles. "Stop worrying. Have a fantastic show, and we'll see you on Saturday. Everything's ready to go. You planned it down to the napkins, remember?"

"And you have the folder? In case anything comes up?"

"I have the folder." He laughs and kisses me on the head. "You never used to be such a worry-wart."

"I want Chloe to have the perfect party."

"She will. Thanks to you."

"Love you," I mutter before his lips close over mine.

"Love you, too, babe."

"You'd never know you've been out of the game for a month," Susan says Friday night after the show. My heart is pumping, my breath coming fast, and I can't wait to get out of this sequined costume.

But damn, it felt good.

"Nothing beats Madison Square Garden," I say before taking a long drink of water. "It's fucking amazing."

"So amazing, we added a second night," she says casually, and I blink at her.

"For Sunday?"

"For tomorrow."

My heart stops. "No. No, Susan, I told you I have to go to New Hope tomorrow."

She sighs and props her hands on her hips. "Scarlett, I just made you an extra three million dollars—that's *your* take—by adding the second night. Not only did people want to honor the tickets they already bought for the show we canceled, but more wanted in. This is not a bad thing. It's *amazing*. People work their whole lives and never experience something like this. You,"—she starts ticking off on her hand—"Beyonce, Garth, and Justin Timberlake are the only ones who come to mind who can pull this off."

"It's amazing," I agree, trying to calm her down. "But I have responsibilities—"

"You're a megastar," she cuts me off coldly. "*This* is your responsibility. And until six weeks ago, you understood that. Now, I'm sorry about your daddy, and I'm so glad that he's made a full recovery. Beyond that, your job is to fucking entertain the people who have given you everything you ever dreamed of."

"I'll finish these last few shows with you," I say, my voice firm, not shaking but angry. "And then we're done."

"Excuse me?"

"You heard me. *I'm* the boss here, Susan, not the other way around. You seem to have forgotten that. Oh, and I went back and looked through my emails. You never sent one. You blindsided me."

"I sent it."

"No. You didn't. Maybe you forgot, and that's okay. I know this is all a lot of work. But I'm not your puppet. I've made you a *very* rich woman, and I'm done. I call the shots, not the other way around, Sue."

"Look, we can work this out."

"I've made up my mind." I shake my head, feeling heartsick and *so damn guilty*. I can't believe I'm going to miss Chloe's party.

Susan stomps out of my green room without another word, and I deflate. Jesus, she's been with me for years. *Years.* I have come to rely on her for so much, and she *is* the boss of most things.

But not of me or my time. Susan booked the second show without even talking to me, without confirming that it would work with *my* schedule. Even after I told her I had to go back home after tonight's show.

I mean, what in the actual fuck?

I check my phone and see that I've missed a call from Tucker. I haven't spoken to him since yesterday morning. When I call, he's not available. And when he calls, I miss it. It's a horrible feeling.

I didn't even get to talk to him last night before I went to sleep.

I press the button to call him and frown when it goes to voice-mail after four rings. It's eleven at night. Where could he be?

"Hey, Tuck. It's me. Give me a call when you get my message."

I change out of my costume but don't bother to take off the makeup. I'll do that at the hotel. Right now, I just want to go back to the room, get a bite to eat, and finally talk with Tucker.

I'm flanked by huge security guards as I'm led out of the building to a limo waiting by the stage door, and less than thirty minutes later, I'm in the presidential suite of the Waldorf.

I strip down and clean my face, brush out my teased hair, and then take a long, hot shower, scrubbing myself clean from head to toe.

Once I'm wrapped in a thick robe, I sit on the sofa and call Tucker again.

"Hey," he says. "Sorry, I was talking with Chloe when you called. She's worried about tomorrow, but I talked her down."

"What is she worried about?"

"Everything," he says with a chuckle. "What if people don't come? What if *you* don't come?"

Sucker-punch to the gut.

"What if someone drowns?"

"Well, that escalated quickly."

"Hey, I'm just the messenger. How are you? How was your show?"

"The show was amazing. It felt really good."

"I'm glad. I'm sure you were fantastic."

"Thanks." I clear my throat. "Uh, Tuck, I have some bad news."

"Don't say it." His voice is soft. "Do *not* tell me you can't come tomorrow."

"I'm so sorry. They booked a second show on me without consulting me. The tickets are sold, it's scheduled, and roughly forty-thousand people are going to show up at Madison Square Garden tomorrow night."

"A little girl is going to show up to her birthday party, one that *you* planned, and she'll be crushed that you aren't there."

"I know." A tear drops down my cheek. "I'm so sorry, Tuck. I was as blindsided as you are, and I fired Susan."

"You fired her?"

"Don't sound so surprised. Yes, I fired her. She fucked with my family, and that won't fly with me. Ever. God, I'm so sorry. I feel awful, and I don't know how to make this up to you both."

"Hey, shit happens, right?"

"No. *This* isn't supposed to happen."

He's quiet, but I can hear him breathing on the other end of the line.

"I'm really sorry," I whisper again.

"I know," he says. But he doesn't say it's okay. Because I know it's *not* okay. I'm as disappointed as he is.

"What can I do?"

"I don't know. I have to tell her. She's going to be crushed."

"But she'll be excited once she gets to the party," I say, trying to put a positive spin on it. "And she's getting a *puppy*. Trust me, as soon as she sees that, she'll be saying, 'Scarlett who?'"

"You're probably right. I have to pick her up tomorrow afternoon. Your dad's going to hide her over at his house, and I guess I'll have Dean pick both Rick and the pup up for the party now."

"Tell Dean I appreciate it."

"I will. Shit, this sucks. I was excited to get my hands on you tomorrow."

"Trust me, I was ready for you to have your hands on me. It's been a long thirty-six-ish hours. How was your day today, anyway?"

"Not fantastic. I had to answer a domestic violence call, and by the time I got there, the asshole had killed his wife *and* himself. It was pretty shitty."

"Oh, God, Tuck. I'm so sorry."

I should be there with him, holding him, letting him vent about the horrible things he saw at work, rather than telling him over the phone that I wouldn't be home tomorrow.

This is not at all how I pictured tonight going.

"Did you know them?" I ask.

"Not well," he admits. "I've been to their house before on similar calls. The guy was a douche. But I couldn't save her, and that weighs on me. You know?"

"Of course, it does. Did they have kids?"

"Thank God, they didn't," he says with a deep sigh. "Listen, babe, I'm going to take a shower and go to bed. I'm exhausted, and it looks like tomorrow's going to be a busy one."

"Okay. I love you."

"Love you, too. Have a good show tomorrow night."

And with that, he's gone, and I'm sitting under a mountain of guilt and anger.

~ TUCKER ~

"She's not coming, is she?"

"I'm sorry, Chlo." I wrap my arm around her shoulders. Chloe doesn't let me hug her often, so when she doesn't immediately pull away, I tighten my grip and relish the moment.

"It's okay." Chloe shrugs and looks at me. "I understand. It's her job."

Damn. I wish I were that nonchalant about it. I'm still pissed. It sounds unreasonable for me to be mad at Scarlett, even to my own ears, but I am. I want her here with us, and a small part of me can't help but wonder if this is how it's always going to be. Missed birthdays, holidays, school programs, and dinners. Will Chloe and I forever come second to Scarlett's career? And what happens if we have our own kid someday? I'm not sure if I can raise another baby on my own.

I guess part of me hoped that since Chloe and I are part of Scarlett's life now, that she would decide to fit us in more. Maybe I was too quick to hope for that grand of a gesture. Or perhaps we just don't mean as much to her as she says we do.

"Dad?"

I shake my head, determined to shelve all thoughts about my situation with Scarlett until after the party. Today is Chloe's day, and I want to focus all of my attention on her. I want this day to be unforgettable, and I'll do whatever I have to do to make that happen.

"Yeah?"

"You okay?"

"Yeah, I'm good. I'm really proud of you, Chlo."

"For what?"

"For being mature about this. I know how bad you wanted Scarlett to be here."

"I guess I'm just finally growing up."

"Not too fast, okay? I'd like to keep you little for a bit longer."

"Sorry, Dad, no can do. I'm almost a woman."

I groan. "Lord, help me."

Chloe laughs. "Come on. I'm ready for my party."

Chloe thinks that we're going early so that she can be there to greet all of her friends. Little does she know that everyone is already there waiting for her. The party wasn't a surprise, but the greeting is going to be.

Mom just texted me that the last kid showed up. Dean, Rick, and Scooter are there with the puppy, which means we need to hit the road.

As long as I don't have to break up any fights, catch any kids kissing in the corner, or save anyone from drowning, tonight will be a success.

"Let's do it."

As SOON AS we walk around the corner, all thirty-five of Chloe's friends and our family jump to their feet and yell, "HAPPY BIRTHDAY!"

Chloe stumbles back, a hand to her chest. She smiles from ear to ear and looks from me to her friends, back to me, and then over to her friends again before running toward them with a high-pitched squeal.

"Did you see her face?" Scooter walks toward me, holding his phone up for me to see the picture he took. "That was priceless. Good job, Dad."

"Will you send that to me?"

Scooter does something on his phone and then looks up. "Done."

Dean joins us, and I look over at where Chloe is stripping off her clothes down to her swimming suit. I make sure she's out of earshot. and then I ask, "Where's the puppy?"

"The little hellion is in the pool house with one of the life-guards," he says, looking down at the teeth marks on the toes of his Chuck T's. "They're going to keep the she-devil until you're ready to give her to Chloe."

Of course, I picked out the ornery puppy. "I'll buy you a new pair."

"Damn right, you will. Those were my favorites."

"Heya, Tucker," Rick says, walking toward us.

"Hey, Rick. You're looking better every time I see you."

He puffs up his chest and smiles. "Thanks. I'm feeling pretty darn good. How's Scarlett?"

I feel my smile start to slip at the mention of her name. "I don't know. I haven't talked to her since late last night."

She was supposed to call this morning, but that didn't happen.

"Yeah." Rick frowns and shakes his head. "She told me she couldn't make it. I know she would be here if she could."

I wish I were as sure about that as he is. "I know."

"Cannonball!"

We all turn in time to see one of the boys in Chloe's class cannonball off the diving board. He splashes all of the girls in the process, causing them to giggle.

"Hold this." Scooter hands me his phone and pulls his shirt over his head.

"What're you doing?"

"I'm gonna show that punk how it's done."

"No, you're not."

"Yes, I am."

"He's twelve."

"So am I—at heart."

"This is gonna be great," Dean says, pulling his phone out and getting ready to record the disaster that's about to happen.

"Go, Scooter!" Chloe yells, tossing her arms into the air. She's floating on a tube in the middle of the pool with Jenny and a few of her other friends surrounding her.

Scooter looks at the boy who just jumped, points to him, and says, "Watch and see how it's done, son."

"Oh, Lord." I roll my eyes.

He climbs onto the diving board, waves to Chloe, and then takes off running. When he gets to the end of the board, he goes to jump, but his foot slips, and he flies through the air and smacks the water face-first.

The entire place starts laughing.

"Please tell me you got that," I say to Dean.

"Every glorious second."

Instinctively, I turn to find Scarlett, to see if she saw, only to remember that she's not here.

Damn it. She should be here, enjoying this, and I can't decide if I'm still upset that she's not, or if I feel sorry for her that she's missing it. We're all laughing and carrying on at a party she worked her ass off to put together, and she's at work, missing all the fun.

I pull my phone from my pocket and send her the photo of Chloe that Scooter sent to me, along with a simple text.

Wish you were here.

I haven't heard from her all day. I thought for sure she would call Chloe this morning to say "happy birthday," or at least send her a text, but she's been completely silent, and I don't know how I feel about that. Has she been busy? If so, what has she been doing? It kills me that we're this far apart, and I know absolutely nothing about her day.

Over the next hour and a half, I send her at least another

dozen photos. Everything from pictures of Chloe and her friends to Scooter making an obscene gesture, and even a photo of Rick sitting on the edge of the pool with his feet dangling in the water.

She doesn't reply to any of them.

Not one.

This is ridiculous. I can't believe I'm spending Chloe's party staring at my phone, waiting on Scarlett. Chloe deserves better than that from me on her birthday, and I deserve better than that, too.

Determined to enjoy the rest of the party without being attached to my phone, I shove it into the pile with Dean's and Scooter's clothes. That way, I can't check my phone every ten minutes without it looking like I'm ogling their underwear, and Scooter would never let me live something like that down.

"Daddy?"

"Yes, sweetheart."

"Can I open my presents now?"

I look around. All of the kids have eaten, and the caterers have cleared out. "I don't see why not."

"Yes!" She fist-pumps the air, then rounds her friends up and digs in. She gets gift cards from most of the boys in her class, and a variety of perfume, clothes, and makeup from the girls.

When she gets to Scooter's present, she tears into it and frowns. "A dog bowl?"

Scooter smiles proudly. "You're welcome."

"Thank you?" She grabs Dean's present and rips it open. She pulls off the top to the box and pulls out a dog leash, dog treats, and a tennis ball. "Uncle Dean, what's all of this for?"

"Ask your dad, kiddo."

She turns to me, eyebrows raised. I signal the lifeguard in the pool house, and she opens the door. Chloe gasps when a tiny ball of fur comes barreling out. The puppy I picked up this morning stumbles twice as she runs across the concrete but gets back up each time. Chloe runs after her and scoops her up.

"Oh. My. Gosh. He's perfect."

"He's actually a she."

"She's perfect," Chloe coos, cuddling the wiggly body to her chest. "But I thought you said I couldn't have a dog."

"Because I wanted it to be a surprise. You're old enough now, and it's time."

With the puppy clutched to her chest, Chloe hugs me. "Thank you. Thank you. Thank you. This is the best birthday present ever. I promise I'll be the best dog mom ever, and I'll train her."

"You'll also be pooper-scooping the yard, taking her out at night, and making sure she stays groomed."

"Yes, yes, and yes. This is amazing, Dad. You're the best."

"Love you, Chlo." I kiss the side of her head and then release her so she can show her new puppy off to her friends.

Everyone crowds around, oohing and ahhing over the newest member of our family.

"You did good, son," Dad says, patting my back.

"Thanks, Dad. I can't believe how fast she's growing up."

Mom steps up to my other side. "Just wait, one of these days, you'll be standing here with Chloe, watching your grandson or granddaughter the way we're watching her."

I smile at my mom and then look at Dad. They're so happy, in love, and content just being here, spending time with their family. That's what I want with Scarlett. When I picture my future, I see the three of us living in the country. Maybe another kid with Scarlett's brown hair, my eyes, and Chloe's smile. I want evenings spent on the porch, watching the sun go down, and Sunday dinners with Rick. But we can't have any of that if Scarlett isn't here.

She should be here, enjoying the moment and making memories. Instead, she's on stage somewhere, entertaining tens of thousands of fans.

"We're going to go, sweetheart," Mom says, pulling me down so she can kiss my cheek. "Tell Scarlett we said hello."

"I will." I hug her and then Dad. "Thanks for coming."

I walk them out and then come back to finish cleaning up. The kids all jump back into the pool, determined to enjoy every last second before it's time to go. Scooter and Dean step in to help me clean, while Rick corrals the puppy.

I pile my arms full of trash and carry it to the garbage can. Voices from the bathhouse catch my attention.

"Can you believe her?" a girl says in a snotty voice. "What a joke."

I dump the trash in the can and scoot a little closer.

"I know," another girl says. "How pathetic? Can you believe she actually told people that Scarlett Kincaid was going to be here?"

The girls laugh, and then I hear another voice. "I overheard her tell a group of people that Scarlett and her dad are dating. No way. If I were her, I'd be embarrassed to show my face in front of my friends."

"You know it's frowned upon to stalk young girls, right?"

I elbow Scooter in the stomach and then pull him to the side. "I'm not stalking the girls. I'm eavesdropping."

"On what? Fifth-grade gossip?"

"They were talking shit about Chloe."

"Bitches," he hisses dramatically.

Damn it. I hate this shit. Girls are so mean these days. "What do I do?"

"You're asking me for advice?"

"You're right. I should talk to Dean."

"Wait." He stops me with a hand to my shoulder. "You want my honest opinion?"

"Yes."

Scooter turns to look at Chloe, and I follow his gaze. She's splashing around with Jenny and a few other girls, laughing and playing.

"You've raised one hell of a girl, Tuck."

"She is pretty great, isn't she?"

"She's more than great. She's funny, smart, and kind. *You* did that, Tuck. You raised that awesome girl, and you should be damn proud. I think you should give yourself a pat on the back. You managed to raise an excellent human being all on your own."

"Not completely on my own. I have you, Dean, and my parents."

"But you did most of the work. She's an awesome person, and while I know you probably want to march in there and give those girls a piece of your mind for bad-mouthing your little girl, I think you should thank your lucky stars that she's not one of them."

He's right. "When did you get so deep?"

He shrugs a shoulder. "I have my moments."

"Thanks, Scooter."

"Anytime, brother. Now, let's go finish cleaning up. I've got a hot date tonight with one of the moms."

"Why does that not surprise me?"

"DAISY IS FINALLY ASLEEP." Chloe drops down on the couch beside me.

"You named her?"

"She looks like a Daisy. Uncle Dean said I should've named her Cruella."

I laugh and shake my head. "I think Daisy is perfect."

"Thanks again for today, it was wonderful."

"You'll have to thank Scarlett. She did ninety-nine percent of the work."

Chloe frowns. "I'm really bummed she couldn't be here."

"I know you are. I think Scarlett would've been here if she could've made it work."

"When will she be home?"

"I honestly don't know, Chlo."

"Can I text her from my phone and say thank you?"

"I think that would be really nice."

Chloe gets up and walks toward the kitchen, but turns around when I call out to her, "Chloe?"

"Yeah?"

"I'm really proud of you. You're blossoming into a wonderful person, and I've really enjoyed watching you grow."

"You mean, I'm blossoming into a wonderful woman?"

"Don't push it. You're still my little girl."

She laughs. "Thanks, Dad. I love you."

"Love you, too, Chloe."

What a day. I close my eyes and drop my head against the couch. I must have dozed off because I wake up sometime later to the shrill sound of my phone ringing. I rub my eyes and look at the clock. It's almost two o'clock in the morning. Who would be calling at this time of night?

I grab my phone and see Scarlett's name flash across the screen. The part of me that misses her like crazy is dying to answer the call and hear her voice. The other part of me, the one that came to a stark realization tonight, hesitates. But I can't *not* answer, that isn't fair to her.

I slide my finger across the screen and answer the call. "Hello?"

"It's so good to hear your voice," Scarlett says, sounding out of breath. "I wasn't sure if you'd answer."

"I'll always answer. You, on the other hand…"

"Wait, are you mad at me?"

"Not mad. Frustrated. Did you even check your phone today?"

"I was busy," she fires back.

"Too busy to send Chloe a happy birthday text, or check in and see how the party was going? Or hell, even to say hi?"

There's a long pause. I prepare myself for the fight and am caught off guard when she apologizes.

"I'm sorry. I'm so sorry. Today was an absolute shitshow. I had interview after interview. I went from one studio to the next, and then to Madison Square Garden. Before I knew it, I was on stage."

"It's two o'clock in the morning."

"I know. The fans were going crazy, and it felt so good to be up there, Tuck. They kept chanting for more, and I had to give them what they wanted."

"What about what I want?"

"Huh?"

"Me, Scarlett. Do you ever think about what I want? Do you even know what I want?" I ask, continuing without giving her a chance to respond. "I just want you…here. I want you here with me and Chloe. I want to wake up to your beautiful face every morning and kiss your sweet lips every night when we go to bed. I want holidays and family reunions, and Christmas concerts. I want a kid with your hair, my eyes, and Chloe's smile."

"Tucker—"

"You were right, we should've talked about this in Nashville because I see now that what I want and what you want are two totally different things. I want laughter and memories, Scarlett. And you want bright lights and screaming fans. Do you even want kids?"

"Don't throw that on me."

"Do you even want me?"

"Of course, I want you."

"Good, because I know that I sure as hell want you. You're it for me, Scarlett. When are you coming home?"

"I don't know. Tomorrow is a travel day because I have a concert on Monday, and then I fly to Austin and then Denver for interviews that had to be rescheduled and—"

"See, this is what I don't want. I can't live my life wondering where you're at each night, and when you're coming home."

"What do you want me to do, Tucker? This is my job."

"I know it is, and I thought I could do this. I thought I could share you with your fans. But, damn it, Scarlett, I don't know if I can."

"What do you want from me? Tell me what you want me to do."

"I want you to choose me."

Scarlett blows out a hard breath. "Are you giving me an ultimatum?"

"I don't know. I don't know what I'm doing. I just know that I can't live like this. I love you more than I will ever love another woman besides Chloe, but I want more out of this. I want more for my life. I want more for *us*. I want to make a family with you and protect you and love you. I want you all of my days, Scarlett, not just some of them."

"I can't do this with you right now, Tucker. Not like this, not over the phone."

"Then, when? When can I see you face-to-face so that we can talk about this?"

"I don't know," she yells. "Look, I've got to go before I say something I'll regret. Goodnight, Tucker."

"Goodbye, Scarlett."

~SCARLETT~

GOODBYE, *Scarlett*.

Two words, repeating in my head over and over again. For a week now. He didn't say goodnight.

He said good*bye*.

And I haven't talked to him since.

We haven't made up, we haven't said, *"we're just frustrated, but it's going to be okay."*

Nada.

Instead, I've spent the past week finishing up the tour and the media circus that surrounds it. I've done countless interviews and have been on television. I've crammed it all into a week so I can take the time I need now to figure out my shitshow of a life.

I landed in Charleston this morning, and I'm driving to New Hope. I gave my dad a heads-up because I'll be staying with him. I don't think I'm welcome at Tucker's right now.

I'm not even sure that Tucker and I are still a thing.

It doesn't feel like it.

It's mid-afternoon when I pull into town, and I immediately feel a sense of deja vu. Has it really been less than two months since the day that Tucker pulled me over on my way into town for the first time? So much has changed since then.

I hadn't been here in a dozen years, and now I can't imagine spending more than a few weeks away.

There's no sign of Tucker as I drive through town and to my dad's place. Tucker shouldn't be home from work yet, which is perfect for me. I'm not ready to see him. And still, I want to see him so badly that it hurts.

Life is complicated.

I glance at Lexi's car parked at the curb and square my shoulders.

This will either be fine or a nightmare.

With my suitcase in tow, I climb the steps to the front door and knock. Dad pulls open the door then me into his arms, giving me a big hug. I'm not ashamed to admit that it makes me want to sob like a baby. There's nothing as good as my dad soothing away something that hurts.

"Hi," I say into his chest and then sniffle loudly.

"Hi, sugar," he says and kisses my head. "Come on in, I'll make you some tea."

"Okay."

I stop when I see Lexi sitting on the couch, watching me with pursed lips.

"You know what, Lexi? I don't have it in me to listen to your nastiness today. So, if you want to lecture me for fucking up a good thing or abandoning everyone or how I'm just generally the spawn of Satan himself, just save it, okay?"

"I'm not Satan," Dad says from the kitchen, making me grin.

"I wasn't going to say any of those things," my sister says, shaking her head. "I was just going to ask how you're doing. Because you look like shit."

"That's appropriate." I sigh and drop into the chair opposite her. "Because I feel like shit."

"I think you need to talk it out," Dad says as he walks in with a steaming mug of tea. He sets it on the table near my elbow and sits in his favorite chair next to mine. "What's going on? Tucker hasn't said much. He just scowls whenever we mention your name."

"Great." I sigh and rub my hands over my forehead. "That's just great. Well, you know I had to miss Chloe's birthday."

"Which was fabulous, by the way," Dad says. "You did a wonderful job planning that party."

"It was the talk of the town," Lexi adds. "I'll let you plan the kids' next birthdays."

I look up in surprise. "You'd let me do that?"

"Of course." She frowns. "I mean, if you want to."

"I would like that," I whisper, embarrassed to be getting emotional. "I was *so* sorry that I had to miss it. I wanted to come home for it more than anything. But things were crazy, and the show got scheduled without me knowing about it. I fired Susan, by the way."

Dad's eyebrows climb in surprise. "She's been your manager since the *Small Town Girl* album."

"And now, she's not," I say with a shrug. "She effed up, and there's no recovering from it for me. I can't trust her."

"Then you did the right thing," Lexi says, surprising me again. Is this *my* sister? The one who can't stand me?

"Thanks. Well, I didn't have time to text or call at all that day, and it pissed Tucker off something fierce. By the time I was able to talk to him late that night, he basically told me he wants way more from me than being an afterthought. That he needs to come before my career, or else he's out."

"He said that?" Dad asks.

"That's the CliffsNotes version. And I haven't talked to him since then. I've texted a couple of times, but he replied with just one word, and that made me feel worse than not hearing anything from him at all, so I stopped. I don't know what he wants from me."

"More," Dad says simply. "Sounds to me like he wants you, not all the pomp and circumstance that comes with you."

"I'm a package deal, just like he and Chloe are a package deal. I *love* her. I would never ask him to choose me over her."

"A career and a child are hardly the same things." They're Lexi's words, but her tone is soft, not accusing or mocking. She's just participating in the conversation. This is the sister I need in my life.

"I understand that," I say. "I do. It's just... I've worked my *ass* off to be where I am with this job. Why should I be the one to give everything up?"

"He's worked hard, too," Dad reminds me. "For his job and raising his daughter by himself. You're not the only one who works hard. He's sacrificed a lot for that little girl."

"I'm not saying I'm the only one who works hard." I shake my head again, feeling misunderstood. "I'm just saying that it seems that we should *both* compromise, not just me. And you don't have to talk to me about sacrifice, Dad. I'm intimate with it. Hell, I feel like I invented it. I've missed *so much* of my family's lives because of my career. I don't have a relationship with my *sister*,"—I point to Lexi, whose eyes fill with tears—"because of my career. So, we can all agree that sacrifice is just a part of life, and compromise is a given when it comes to working through issues with someone you love."

"I agree with you there," Lexi says. "I mean, relationships *are* all about compromise, and maybe that's something I haven't been very good at when it comes to *our* relationship. We'll come back to that later. But I have no suggestions for you with Tucker because your career is in Nashville, and his is here. His daughter's community is here. Everything they know and love, aside from you, is here."

"It's impossible." I look at both of them, waiting for them to disagree, but they don't. "There's no way to make this work. It's just...*done.*"

I hear Tucker's door slam next door, and I stand. "Might as well get this over with."

"Maybe you should take some time to calm down," Dad suggests, but I shake my head.

"It's like yanking off a Band-Aid." I push out of the front door, then march down the steps and over to Tucker's house. I knock on the door. Tucker's eyes light up when he sees me on the other side, and, God, I want to launch myself into his arms. I want to tell him that I'm sorry, beg for his forgiveness, and rip off his clothes.

But what's the point?

We can't make this work.

"Hey, Scar. I wasn't expecting you." He steps back, letting me inside. "Chloe's at Jenny's."

He blinks like he doesn't know why he said that, but I'm glad he did because I'd rather not do this in front of a twelve-year-old.

"That's okay," I reply stiffly and stand inside the door. "I won't keep you long."

"What are you talking about? When did you get to town?"

"Just about an hour ago." Hurt flashes through his eyes, and I hate myself even more. "I wasn't sure that you'd want to see me."

"Are you kidding me? I'll always—"

"Just listen, okay? You did a lot of talking last week, now it's my turn."

"Okay." He crosses his arms over his chest and watches me with an impassive face. "Go ahead."

"You were right," I begin, hating every damn word coming from my mouth. "This isn't going to work."

I don't know how to make it work.

"I mean, we're great together. I love you so much. And Chloe, too. But I also love my career. I don't want to give it up, and you don't want to bend either, to work it out. You want so many wonderful things, and I just don't see how I can give them to you. I *promised* you that I'd be here last weekend, and I couldn't make that happen. I felt like shit. I still do. It wrecked me. And it hurt both you and Chloe. You're right, it might happen again, probably more than once. Because my life is crazy. I don't live in a sleepy little town where everyone knows everyone, and you fall in love and get married and have a quiet life. That's just not me."

I hold my hands out at my sides as if to say, *"what can I do?"*

Tucker takes a hesitant step forward, panic and desperation flashing in his eyes.

"But that *is* you, Tuck. That's so you. You deserve all of the Sunday dinners and evenings on the porch swing. Babies and dogs and a life that fulfills you."

Tucker's eyes grow suspiciously glossy, and I'm tempted to throw myself into his arms and tell him that everything I just said was a lie. But that would only hurt us more in the long run. And I don't want to hurt Tucker any more than I already have.

I have to swallow hard over the words I'm about to say next because, God, I don't want to say them. It's just about killing me.

"Someone can give you that," I whisper, my throat hoarse. "But she's not me. And we both know it."

"So, you're just going to walk away? Throw in the towel?"

"What else am I supposed to do?" I watch him for a long moment, wanting to reach out for him, but that would be cruel to both of us. So, I turn to go. But before I can even reach for the door, I'm spun around and pinned to it, and Tucker has my jawline in his hands and is kissing me for all he's worth, pressing that hard body of his against mine, making me come alive from head to toe in the way only he can.

When neither of us can breathe anymore, he pulls away and watches me with hot eyes, panting.

"Don't leave, not like this."

"It's too late, Tucker, I'm already gone."

I cover my lips with my fingertips. And, without another word, I walk through the door.

It's been three days since I walked away from Tucker. Three days of confusion, tears, and anger. Three days of wishing I could have a do-over and wondering what the heck I would say if that wish came true. Three days of trying to figure out how to move on with my life when all I want is to be with Tucker: in his home, in his life, in his arms.

I'm sitting in the kitchen with my guitar in my lap, strumming through the fourth song I've written since I walked away from him. Apparently, what I said to Chase weeks ago is true. I may not end up with Tucker, but I might get a hit single—or four—out of our breakup.

Sure, every song is sappy and describes in one way or another how much I miss him. And love him, and hate him, and miss him. Did I mention that I miss him?

More than once, I've found myself picking up the phone to call him and Chloe, only to remember that I no longer have that privilege. And rather than find a way to fix our mess, I simply gave up. But as the minutes turned into hours, and the scribbled words on paper turned into songs, I started to formulate a plan.

"Goddamn water heater," Dad grumbles as he walks into the kitchen.

"What's wrong?" I ask, setting my guitar to the side.

"The pilot light keeps going out," he says. "The damn thing is fifteen years old. I should replace it."

"Why didn't we replace it when you had all the work done five years ago?"

"It wasn't fifteen years old then," he says calmly. "And at the end of the day, this place is getting older. Things are going wrong, one by one. The roof will need to be re-shingled this fall."

"Why didn't I know any of this?"

He glances at me, and I know why.

Because I'm never here.

"You need a new house," I say, getting Dad's attention. "And, no, I'm not suggesting you move away from New Hope. We just need to get you a new house here."

"Or we can buy a new hot water heater and fix the roof."

"That's not fun." I stand, propping my hands on my hips.

"And I have an idea. It sort of came to me when I was writing this morning."

"Let's hear it."

"Well, Dad, remember when you said being an overachiever runs in the family?"

"Sure."

"I've been thinking about Tucker a lot, and about what you and Lexi said."

Dad turns fully toward me. "Glad to hear it, but what does that have to do with being an overachiever?"

"I don't like the idea of giving up on Tucker. I *love* him, Daddy." Dad grins as if he knew this would be where this would go all along, and *I'm* just now catching up. "I'm not a quitter. When I know what I want, I chase after it, even when it's hard. And I *want* Tucker so much I ache with it."

These last few days without him have made that realization increasingly clear. I thought I could walk away from him and what we have, but I can't. I don't want to.

What I want is Tucker.

My heart rate kicks up at the thought of getting him back.

"So, what's your plan, sugar?"

"I'm making it up as I go, but I love New Hope, not just Tucker. This is home for me. It took coming back to realize that, but I get it now. I'll have to go to Nashville from time to time, and there will still be tours and such, but I think I can work it out where I'll spend a good deal of the year here."

Dad's eyes light up with hope.

"I'd like to buy some property, and build two, maybe three houses on it. One for Tucker, Chloe, and me, one for you, and if she wants it, one for Lexi and the family."

"It'll have to be a big piece of property," Dad says, rubbing his chin. "Because that's a lot of people living in one place."

"If I bought like five hundred acres, there would be plenty of room."

He raises a brow. "Can you afford something like that?"

I smile and wrap my arms around my father. "Daddy, I have more than enough money for this."

"Okay, but I still don't understand what this has to do with being an overachiever."

"I'm going to win Tucker back. I'm going to prove to him that I'm serious about us. That this isn't just another empty promise with no results. If I buy property, build homes, set down roots in New Hope, maybe I'll convince him that we can both bend to make this work. I'll only schedule tours in the summer when we can travel as a family, and try to be here for the rest of the time. I don't have the particulars figured out, obviously, but it's way better than where I was three days ago."

"Why don't you just walk your ass over to his house and tell him you want him back and get on with your lives?"

I shake my head. "I can't. I've failed him, more than once. My word means nothing to him right now. So, I'm going to show him."

"Building a house is a long process. What if during that time, he meets someone else and moves on?" Dad suggests.

My heart stops. I never considered that. "Do you really think that could happen?"

Dad scoffs. "No. That boy is crazy about you."

"Geez, Dad, you about gave me a heart attack. You can't say things like that to me."

"Love is wasted on the young," Dad says, shaking his head.

"Is that a yes? Do you like my plan?"

"What if I say no?"

"I'll just talk you into it."

"That's what I thought."

"This is the property."

After I made my mind up yesterday, I got to work hiring a real estate agent, and I called Lexi and Jason over for a family meeting.

It was an evening of laughter and plans, and for the first time that I could remember, it felt like we were a real family.

"Are you sure?" Dad asks as we stare out over the fields. "The view sure is pretty."

"There's a river about a quarter of a mile that way," Chuck, the real estate agent I hired, says. "And a small lake over to the right. They have a tendency to be swampy now, but you can have it all cleaned out, get rid of the gators and such, and it would be quite lovely."

"We can't have gators," I agree, shaking my head. "But a lovely lake would be great. I'm adding a pool area to my house that everyone can use whenever they like."

"The kids will love that," Dad says with a smile. "And I might take a dip or two myself."

"This is it," I say again. "How much does Mr. Truman want again?"

Chuck rattles off a number that has Dad's eyes widening, but I just shake my head. "Take a hundred K off that and make the offer. He's priced it way too high. I'll pay cash."

"I'll write up the offer today, and keep you posted."

"Thanks, Chuck."

"My pleasure."

"We'll stay for just a few moments, if you don't mind."

"Help yourselves," Chuck says with a smile. "I'll be in touch soon."

He drives away, and Dad and I smile at each other. "Looks like you just bought yourself three hundred acres, sugar."

"If old man Truman takes my offer."

"He will." Dad takes my hand and gives it a squeeze. "I have a good feeling about it."

"Would you like a waterfront house?" I ask him.

"Nah, I don't like gators either. Let's stick to the meadow."

"Deal."

"When are you going to tell Tucker?"

"I already told you, I'm not telling him anything. I'm showing him."

Dad shakes his head and walks to the car. "Put that poor boy out of his misery."

"I'm working on it. But you gotta admit, this is a pretty great plan."

"It's a wonderful plan. Tucker's a lucky guy."

"I'll be the lucky one, just as soon as I get him back."

~ TUCKER ~

I TIP my head back and cringe as the whiskey burns a path down my throat.

"One more," I say, putting the shot glass on the bar.

Scooter takes the shot glass and eyes me warily. "You sure?"

"Scooter, that was my first one."

"But you usually don't do shots. I'm just looking out for you."

"I don't need you to look out for me, I need you to pour me another shot."

He lifts a brow and looks at Dean but does as I ask.

"I take it you haven't talked to Scarlett," Dean says.

"Not since she left me." And now, I'm a miserable fuck. I never thought I'd be the type of man to pine over a woman, but that's exactly what I've been doing. Even Chloe doesn't want to be around me.

Scooter slides the full shot glass to me, and I toss it back. I hand him the glass and lean my elbows on the bar.

"I contacted the Nashville P.D."

It wasn't an easy decision to make, but it was the right one because I can't live without Scarlett. She's it for me, and if she isn't willing to bend, then I have to be.

Scooter's jaw drops open.

Dean scowls. "Why the fuck would you do that?"

"Because I love her."

"So, you're just going to leave? What about me, and Mom and Dad, and Chloe's friends, and—?"

"And me," Scooter inserts.

"What does Chloe think about this?" Dean asks, flustered at the bomb I just dropped.

"She doesn't know. I didn't want to say anything until I heard back from them."

"*Have* you heard back from them?"

I look at Dean and nod. "I'm scheduled for a phone interview next week. If that goes well, I'll make a trip out there for a face-to-face interview."

"Fuck." Dean pushes his hands into his hair.

"For the record, I think you're doing the right thing."

"Thank you, Scooter."

He nods. "Have you told Scarlett?"

"Not yet. I didn't want to get her hopes up. I might not get the job."

"You'll get the job," Dean says with an air of confidence. "You're a damn fine police officer."

"Don't you think you should run this by Scarlett first? What if you take the job and move there, and then she doesn't take you back?"

Damn. I never even considered that option. "I'll have to think it over. I didn't say my plan was foolproof."

"What's up, gentlemen?" Chuck says, sliding onto a barstool on the other side of Dean. He was four years older than us in school and is a regular here at Scooter's.

"How are ya, Chuck?" Dean says, shaking his hand.

"I'm great." He smiles brightly and points at Scooter. "I'll have a Bud Light, and one for these fine men, too."

"Thanks," Dean says.

"What's the occasion," I ask as Scooter slides a beer to each of us.

"I just closed a massive sale."

"Oh, yeah?" Dean looks from Chuck to me and back to Chuck. "What sold?"

I snap my fingers. "Was it that old building on twenty-third? I hope whoever bought it, tears it down. That thing is an eyesore."

Chuck shakes his head. "Nope. I just sold the old Truman place."

"Bill Truman?" Dean clarifies.

"The one and only."

I take a drink of my beer. "That place has been for sale for years."

"Trust me, I know. No one wanted to buy it because he was asking way too much."

"It's a damn fine piece of property," Dean says.

"It sure is, and all it took was the right buyer with deep enough pockets."

"Who in this town, other than Truman himself, can afford to pay that kind of money?" I ask.

"Scarlett Kincaid, that's who." Chuck tips his beer toward us and takes a swig, while mine spews from my mouth.

"Damn it, Tucker." Scooter tosses me a rag to clean up the mess, but all I can do is stare at Chuck.

"Scarlett bought the acreage?" That's impossible. She has no interest in living here. The Truman place is made for all of the things that I want in life, stuff that she made it clear she has no interest in.

Chuck nods. "Wrote a check and signed the papers today. It's official."

"What the hell is she going to do with three hundred acres?" I ask, trying to wrap my head around this new piece of information.

And why didn't she tell me that she was buying it?

Maybe because she really is done with me. The thought is like a punch to the gut. And to think that I was about to uproot my family and my life to be near her.

"She talks like she's going to build a big ol' house."

"Great." I drain the rest of my beer and slam it down.

"Easy," Scooter warns.

I give him an apologetic look and lower my head to my hands. The last thirteen years have been hard enough, thinking about her and missing her, knowing she wasn't around. How am I supposed to live in the same town as her and not want to be with her? And what happens when she decides to start dating?

The thought alone has my blood pumping and causes a twitch to start up in my eye. I'm going to end up in prison for murder because that's what I'll do—I'll kill any man who even tries to touch her.

I've gotta get out of here and go somewhere quiet where I can think about what I want to do. I pull my wallet out of my back pocket, toss a twenty on the bar top, and slide off the stool.

"Where are you going?" Dean asks.

"Home. I need to think."

"I'll drive you."

"No need. I'm fine."

Scooter doesn't say a word, but one look at him, and I know that *he* knows how badly I'm hurting.

I drive home in a Scarlett-induced fog, every possible scenario of what she could be doing racing through my head. It's well after three o'clock in the morning before I fall asleep, and I'm up again at the ass crack of dawn.

Chloe had a slumber party for Lizzie's birthday, and I don't have to pick her up until much later, so I move around the house doing busy work. I mow the lawn, clean the gutters, trim the bushes, and wash my car, all while keeping a close eye on Rick's house, hoping for a glimpse of Scarlett.

I know she hasn't left because her rental is still in the drive-way, and I'm determined to be here when she comes outside. And when she does, I'm going to corner her and find out what in the world is going on. She can't stay cooped up in Rick's house all day.

I watch and wait and wait some more and an hour before I'm due to pick up Chloe, I dart in the house and take a quick shower. When I walk back outside, Scarlett's car is gone.

"Son of a bitch."

If I didn't know better, I'd think that she was waiting for me to go inside before leaving.

"That's it," I mumble marching across the yard.

I bang on the door twice, and it flings open. Rick smiles at me.

"Where's Scarlett?"

"Nice to see you, too, Tucker."

"Sorry." I drop my head and sigh. "Hello, Rick. You're looking great. How's life?"

"Not too shabby, thanks for asking."

I nod. "Good to hear it. Where's your daughter?"

"I imagine Lexi is with the kids. She's probably at home if you need to talk to her."

I stare at him blandly. "You know I'm not asking about Lexi."

"Oh," he says dramatically. "You mean Scarlett. She just left."

"Where did she go?"

"Alfonzo's."

"The Italian restaurant? Who did she go there with?"

"Uhh…" Rick's smile falters. "A friend. She went with a friend."

"Scarlett doesn't have any friends here."

"She made a new one."

He's lying through his teeth. "Really? What's her name?"

"Damn it, Tuck." Rick drags a hand through his hair. "I can't lie for shit. She's at Alfonzo's with Dawson Peterson."

I flinch back. "Dawson Peterson?"

What the hell would she be doing with Dawson Peterson? Sure, he has lots of money and his own business, but—

"Wait. Are they on a date?" I'll kill him with my bare hands if he so much as touches her.

"No, nothing like that."

"Then, what is it?" I shake my head and step off his porch. "I can't believe this. I can't believe that I was ready to take a job in Nashville to be with her and here she is buying land, going on dates, and living her life as though our relationship didn't just end."

"Wait, you know about the land purchase?" Rick asks. "Did Scarlett tell you about it?"

"No. Chuck came into Scooter's last night, bragging about it."

"Oh."

"Why?"

"No reason. I was just curious."

I turn to Rick and look at him pleadingly. "What's going on, Rick? Is she moving on for good? Is that what's happening? Because I don't know if I can do this. How am I supposed to watch her move on with her life, knowing it doesn't include me? It'll fucking kill me."

Rick frowns. "You need to talk to her, son."

"Why do you think I'm here? I stood outside all morning and half of the afternoon, waiting to see her, and the second I stepped inside, she disappeared. Obviously, she doesn't want to see me. Christ, I'm such an idiot."

I turn away, and Rick calls out to me. "Where are you going?"

"I have to go get Chloe." And then I'm going to call the Nashville P.D. and tell them to pull my application because I refuse to chase a woman who doesn't want to be pursued.

"ARE YOU OKAY, DAD?" Chloe asks, climbing into the car. She tosses her backpack into the back seat, buckles up, and looks at me.

"Yeah. Why wouldn't I be?"

"I don't know, you tell me. You look like shit."

I give her a hard look. "Language."

"Sorry." She blanches and then tries to offer me that innocent-little-girl smile. "So, what gives?"

"I'm fine."

"Right. And I'm Taylor Swift." Chloe's phone vibrates in her bag, and she reaches back to pull it out. I started letting her take it to sleepovers in case she needs to call me to come and get her, but only with the understanding that I have access to her texts and pictures when she gets back.

"Who's that?" I ask.

"Scarlett," she says, causing my heart to skip a beat.

"Scarlett is texting you?"

"Uh-huh." Chloe finishes whatever it is she's typing and puts her phone down. "She texts me every day."

Well, isn't that just great? She loves my daughter enough to text her but can't bother reaching out to me. Is the woman trying to drive me out of my mind? Because she is, and she's ripping my heart out in the process.

"Would it be okay if I spend some time with her tomorrow?"

"For what?"

Is it pathetic that I'm jealous of my own daughter?

I shouldn't be that way. I should be happy that Chloe has a woman in her life that she can trust and enjoys spending time with.

"Just to hang out. I miss her."

Me, too! "I guess. Is she going to pick you up?"

"Yep. Thanks, Dad." She types out another text, presumably to Scarlett, and then turns up the radio.

On our way through town, I see Dawson Peterson's truck pulling into a parking space outside of his office building. I whip my car to the left, take the spot beside him, and open the door.

"Stay here, Chloe, I'll be right back."

"Where are you going?"

"Just need to talk to someone real quick."

She shrugs, and I shut the car door. When I walk through the front door of Dawson's building, a bell chimes, signaling my entry. A second later, he walks out of his office and smiles at me.

"Hey, Tucker. Long time no see."

He holds out his hand for me to shake, and when I take it, I pull him close with enough force for him to realize that I'm not here for a friendly visit. I have to be careful about how aggressive I get because I'm a town cop, but I can still let the guy know I mean business.

"W-what are you doing?" he stutters.

"If you hurt her, I will break every bone in your body."

His eyes grow big. "Hurt who?"

"Scarlett. She's special, and she deserves someone who is going to treat her like gold, and that someone isn't you, it's me. She can't see that right now because she has her head stuck so far up her ass, but that woman is mine."

Dawson is shaking his head furiously and trying to back away, but I won't let him. "I'm not with Scarlett."

"You had lunch with her today."

"It was strictly business, I swear."

I loosen my grip but don't let him go. "What business could you possibly have with her?"

"She hired me to build her house."

"She…what?" I release my hold, and Dawson takes two giant steps back, his hands in the air.

"I'm going to build her and Rick's houses."

"She's building a house," I say, to no one in particular.

"And Rick's. Maybe even Lexi's, but I haven't been contracted for that one yet. Our lunch today was to go over the contract."

So, it's true. She's moving back. The love of my life wouldn't move back here for me, but she's willing to do it now that we're no longer together. A sharp pain rips through my chest. I reach up to rub the offending ache and walk toward the door.

"You okay, Tucker?"

"Sorry for bothering you, Dawson."

"No problem. You're in love, and it makes us do crazy things."

"Yeah, I'm in love. But clearly, she's not."

~ S C A R L E T T ~

"So, what did you think of the property?" I ask Chloe as we drive back to town. I pull into Charlie's Diner and put the car in park.

"It's *so* pretty. And it's out of town, but not *too* far from town, you know?"

"That's what I thought, too." We climb out of the car and walk inside. Once we're seated in a booth, I pull my iPad out of my handbag and bring it to life. "I have more things to show you."

"Awesome." We pause to place our orders—two burgers, fries, and chocolate shakes thank you very much—and then we lean over the table, looking at the screen of my iPad. "Are these house plans?"

"Yep. I have a couple that are my favorites, but I want your opinion."

"Cool." I walk her through each one like we're walking through them in real life. "So, the laundry is downstairs?" she asks with a frown. "But the bedrooms are upstairs. That's a pain in the butt. We have that now, and the laundry is heavy."

"You have a really good point," I reply, considering it and not admitting that I haven't done my own laundry in a decade. But no one wants to carry heavy baskets of laundry up stairs. The waitress sets our shakes in front of us. "So, we need a laundry room on the same floor as the bedrooms."

"That would be easiest," she agrees. "Wow, your house is going to be *awesome*. I'm so excited you decided to move here."

"Thanks. And can I tell you a secret?"

"Duh." She grins and spoons some chocolate shake into her mouth.

"I'm hoping this won't be just *my* house. My goal is for you and your dad to live there with me."

"Seriously?"

"Yeah, but you can't tell your dad because it's a surprise."

"I won't tell him. Oh my God, this is *so* amazing. Can I decorate my room?"

"Of course, you can. And you can help me decorate the rest of the house, too."

"So cool," she says again just as her phone pings with a text. "That's Dad. *Where are you? You've been gone a long time.* Geez, he's been so grouchy lately."

I frown and sip my shake. "Really?"

"Like, beyond grouchy," she confirms and types out something to her dad. "And he's mopey. Like I am when something makes me sad."

Well, damn. I guess in my haste to form a plan to get him back, I didn't consider that, in the meantime, Tucker would be heartbroken.

I'm a total bitch. That should have been the first thing on my mind.

"I'm sorry he's been hard to live with. That's my fault."

Our meals are delivered, and Chloe digs into her fries. "Did you guys break up or something?"

"Yeah." I sigh and fiddle with a fry, suddenly no longer hungry. "I'm a horrible person."

"No, you're not. You're planning on building homes for your entire family, not to mention for a kid who isn't even *your* kid.

You're just excited, and you have tunnel vision. That's what Dad calls it when I do that."

"Your dad's pretty smart."

"Yeah, he's just been on my last nerve this week."

She licks some ketchup off her finger.

"Chlo, whether or not I'm able to clean this mess up, and your dad and I get back together again, I want you to know that I love you very much. And I'll always be your friend, no matter what."

"I know." God, is it this easy for kids? "We're cool, Scar. But if you and Dad *do* get back together and get married, I could call you Mom. You know…maybe someday."

I blink at the sudden onslaught of emotion caught in my chest.

"I mean, sure. If you want to."

She smiles happily. "Awesome. You've been so good for Dad. He smiles so much more since you've been home, and he laughs a lot. He didn't always do that. I think he was just stressed out because I'm a handful."

I bark out a laugh and sip my shake. "I don't think you're a handful."

"Oh, I am." She nods wisely. "And he has a pretty important job. People here really respect him."

"I know."

And I was pushing to tear him away from all of this.

I'm a selfish person.

"But you make him happy. And you're nice to me, not just because you have to be to impress my dad, but because you like me."

"I like you very much."

"I like you, too." She smiles as her phone pings again. "Geez, Dad, calm down."

"Maybe we should get you home."

"Yeah, you'd think I'd been abducted by a serial killer. He's so lame."

I laugh again. She was just singing his praises, and now he's lame. I guess that's how it goes when you're a kid.

I ask for a box for all of our uneaten food, pay the tab, and we set off for home. When I pull into the driveway, I see Dad on the porch.

"Hey, Chloe," he says when we step out of the car. He looks at me with a grim nod. "Why don't you come hang out with me for a while so Scarlett can go chat with your dad?"

"Cool," Chloe says.

"Go share some of that food with Rick," I say with a smile. "But save some fries for me."

"Okay," she says as she hurries up to the house and they disappear inside. I walk over to Tuck's and knock on the door.

"Where's Chloe?" he asks when he opens the door.

"She's with my dad, eating my lunch."

He nods. "Okay, just send her over when she's done."

"Hey, Tuck, I'd like to chat with you, if that's okay."

"*Now* she wants to chat," he mutters as he steps back, letting me inside. "It's about damn time because I've had half of the town filling me in on what you're doing, and I'm at a complete loss."

I frown. "Damn small towns."

He just watches me with hurt eyes, and I know without a doubt that I have to fix this. *Right now.*

"So, I came up with a plan." I have to pace his living room. I can't stand still. "After we spoke last week, I was just so sad, so heartsick. Because I don't want to be without you, Tuck. I just love you and Chloe so much, I figured there *has* to be a way to work it out. And then Dad's house started crumbling around me, and I was like…you need a new house."

"Rick's house is crumbling?"

"Let me get this out."

Tucker holds up his hands in surrender, and I keep going.

"So, I thought, what if I build a house here in New Hope? Because I love it here so much, and I didn't know how much I missed it until I was back again. And if I build a house, I could build Dad a guest house on the property. And if I'm gonna do all that, I might as well build Lexi and Jason a house, too."

"That's a lot of houses."

I give him the stink-eye, and he stops talking, but the corners of his lips turn up, which is encouraging.

"I couldn't just march over here and say, '*never mind everything I said the other day. I'll move home, and we'll be together.*'"

"Why? That actually sounds really good. I would've liked that a lot."

"Because they're just words, Tuck. I've made you too many promises that I had to break. Words don't mean anything. *Actions* do. So, I decided to build the house, and show you that I'm serious about planting roots in New Hope. I know we'll still have to work out how touring works, and all of the other craziness that is my career, but I can be based out of South Carolina. There's no rule that says I have to live in Nashville if I'm a country star."

"You do realize that the house can take up to two years to be built?" he says. "So, were you going to just wait around for two years to fill me in on your plan?"

"I hadn't gotten that far yet," I confess and bite my lip. "I mean, probably not, because I *really* miss you and I think about you every second of every day, but I had to have something in place to prove to you that I'm willing to do my part to bend to make this work. I can compromise. I love you, Tuck. I don't want to just throw that away."

Finally, *finally,* he sweeps me up in his arms and kisses me like his life depends on it. And for the first time in weeks, the knot in my belly loosens.

"I've been a wreck," he confesses when he comes up for air. "I almost beat the shit out of Dawson because I thought he took you out on a date."

"What? No, I'm not dating him. He's going to build the houses."

"I know that now. It was just making me crazy that you were planning to move here but not be in my life. How was I supposed to see you all the time and not touch you? Not *love* you?"

"So, my plan had holes."

"A few, yeah."

"Chloe knows," I confess with a smile.

"My own *daughter* was in on the plan?"

"Only as of about an hour ago," I reply. "And she's kind of excited at the thought of decorating her own room. If you forgive me, that is."

"I thought the kissing thing kind of implied that I forgave you."

I cup his face in my hands. "I love you, Tucker Andrews."

"I love you, even though you make me crazy. Being married to you won't be boring."

I freeze. "*Married*?"

"Oh, babe. If you think I'm not putting a rock on that finger, you're the crazy one. You're mine, from now until the end of time. And, frankly, I don't give two fucks if we live in New Hope or Nashville, as long as we're together."

"We might be living in both places from time to time."

"We'll figure it out," he says, his mouth hovering over mine. "It's all about compromise, you know?"

EPILOGUE

~ Tucker ~

"Hey, Tucker, how are you?"

"I'm good, how are you, Dave?" I say to the stage manager as he strides by.

"As good as I can be. It's going to be a long few days."

"You wouldn't have it any other way."

We're kicking off the Home Again tour. Five cities and five concerts over the next five days.

"You're right." He laughs and keeps walking.

It's taken us almost three years to work out a routine, but Scarlett, Chloe, and I have finally found a groove that works. As promised, Scarlett has limited her tours to summers only, and Chloe goes with her from start to finish. I'm not quite as lucky due to my work schedule, but I've been able to work it out where I spend the majority of the summer with them. When I do have to go home to New Hope to work a few shifts, we hire extra staff to make sure there's always someone watching over Chloe, and she wouldn't have it any other way. She loves being on tour with Scarlett.

From August until May, Scarlett is home in New Hope with

us. She has to leave from time to time for interviews or TV appearances, but she's never gone for longer than a few days, and sometimes, we go with her. Lexi and her kids have even gone with Scarlett a couple of times.

I'm on cloud nine. When Scarlett and I got back together three years ago, I didn't think that life could get much better, and then she married me, and I was proven wrong. Life got more than better. I pinch myself every morning as a reminder that I'm not dreaming. I've got a beautiful, talented wife, a wonderful, smart daughter, and a career that I love. Sure, life gets hectic from time to time, but with my girls by my side, I wouldn't have it any other way.

"Hey, Chloe. Where's your mom?"

"In her dressing room, why?"

"Larry needs her to come down to the stage so he can fit her harness." Scarlett is still using a harness and zip line to fly across the stage as part of a stunt during her show. She does it at every concert, and her fans love it.

I kiss Chloe's head and keep walking down the long corridor to Scarlett's dressing room. I knock twice and walk in.

"I could've been naked," she says, perched on a stool in front of her vanity.

"You know better than to leave the door unlocked if you're naked."

"I love it when you get all possessive." She giggles and pulls me down for a kiss.

My hands slide down her sides as I deepen the embrace and then remember that I came in here for a reason. If we don't stop now, I'm going to have her stripped naked and my cock buried in her tight body. Then she'll be late for the show, and it'll be my fault, and we don't need a mess like that again.

Scarlett pouts when I pull away from her. "I wasn't done."

"I promise that I'll ravish every inch of you tonight, but right now, Larry needs you down at the stage so he can fit you for the harness."

"Oh." Her lips part, and then she shrugs a shoulder. "I, uh, I'm not going to need the harness for this tour."

"Why not?"

"Because I'm not doing the stunt."

"But you always do the stunt. Your fans expect it, and it's something that you love to do."

She nods and bites her bottom lip. "You're right, I do love it, but my doctor said it isn't safe for me to do anymore now that I'm...pregnant."

"Your doctor—*wait*. What did you say?"

"I'm pregnant."

"You're pregnant?"

Scarlett nods.

"I'm going to be a father again?"

"Pretty sure that's how it works."

I pull Scarlett into my arms and cup her face. "You're pregnant with my baby," I whisper against her lips, trying desperately not to cry.

"I found out this morning."

"How far along are you?"

"Eight weeks. I don't really want to tell anyone until we hit the twelve-week mark, if that's okay."

"That's more than okay."

Scarlett squeals when I lift her up and twirl her around.

"You have made me the happiest man in the world. And Chloe is going to be so excited."

"I can't wait to tell her. She's going to be the best big sister."

"And you're going to be the best mom." I kiss Scarlett, deeply and passionately before dropping to my knees.

I pull her shirt up and press my lips to her belly. Scarlett slides her fingers into my hair, holding me against her.

"I can't believe this is happening. I've dreamed of this moment so much over the last few years."

"Believe it, babe. In roughly thirty-two weeks, we'll be the parents of a beautiful baby girl or boy."

Thirty-one and a half weeks later

"I hate you." Scarlett's face contorts in pain as she grips my hand with a strength I didn't know she was capable of. "You did this to me."

"You're doing great, sweetheart. You're almost there."

The pregnancy went relatively smooth. Scarlett had some morning sickness early on, but other than that, she had an uneventful pregnancy. The delivery, on the other hand, hasn't been quite so easy.

We're going on eighteen hours of labor, and I'm not sure how much more my girl can take. She looks absolutely exhausted, but I refuse to let her give up. She can yell, curse me, call me every name in the book, and I'll stay right by her side and get her through this.

"Almost there? I'm trying to push a watermelon out of my vagina!" she yells between the contractions.

"I need another big push from you, Scarlett," Dr. Halpert says from her spot between my wife's legs.

I look down and see the top of our baby's head along with a tuft of black hair, and already, my heart is swollen with so much love I want to burst.

"Baby, I can see her head. She has a thick mop of dark hair."

"It's not a sheeeeeeee," Scarlett moans as the wave on the monitor goes higher and higher. "It's a he. *Oh, God, this hurts*. It hurts so bad, Tuck, make it stop. Please, make it stop. I promise I'll do anything, just get me out of here."

"We're not going anywhere without our baby."

We opted not to find out what we're having. I said from day one that I think it's a girl, and Scarlett swears it's a boy. Chloe doesn't care what it is.

Dr. Halpert watches the monitor and prepares for the next big contraction. "Here we go, Scarlett. Same thing you've been doing for me. Bear down and give me a big push. Now, Scarlett. *Push. Push. Push.*"

I hold Scarlett's foot, helping keep her knee raised while my other hand stays clenched in hers.

She grits her teeth, bears down, and a deep growl rips from her chest.

"Yes, baby, yes! Keep going, she's almost here."

Scarlett sucks in a quick breath and bears down once more. This time, the head slides out, followed by a slimy body. I do a quick scan.

Ten fingers.

Ten toes.

One penis.

A penis.

My baby has a penis.

"It's a boy!" I announce, turning to my beautiful wife. "Oh, Scarlett, you gave me the most perfect little boy."

The doctor hands our sweet boy to Scarlett, and she cradles his tiny body to her chest. He's screaming, and she's sobbing, and now I'm crying.

"He's beautiful."

"Just like you." I kiss her sweaty forehead and lean down to get a better look at our son. "He has your nose."

"And your lips."

"And your dark hair."

"He looks just like Chloe!" she says, laughing while crying. "Will you go get Chloe? I want her here with us."

I nod toward the nurse. She told me earlier that she'd go get Chloe from the waiting room as soon as we gave her the okay. Scarlett offered for Chloe to be in here for the delivery, but she politely declined. "There are just some things I'm not ready to see," our daughter said.

Another nurse walks up and reaches for the baby. "Scarlett, we're going to take the baby just for a few minutes, and then we'll hand him right back, and you can feed him."

"Okay."

I stay by Scarlett's side and watch them clean our little guy up. He finally stops fussing, and I swear he looks at me from across the room. I probably look like a giant blob because his eyesight is shit right now, but all I can do is stare back at him. He's so—

"He's perfect," Chloe croons, stealing the words right out of my head as she rushes into the room. She hugs me and then goes straight for her mom.

If you didn't know any better, you'd swear that Scarlett is Chloe's biological mother. She treats her as though she's her own, and I couldn't be more grateful for that. It takes a special kind of woman to take on someone else's child, and Scarlett is the very best kind of extraordinary.

"Have you picked out a name yet?"

Scarlett and I shake our heads.

"We're torn between two names. I like Daniel, and your dad likes Aaron."

Chloe walks across the room where our baby boy is lying on the table, fussing. The nurses are doing whatever it is they do, and Chloe sticks an arm through the action and touches her brother's hand. He instantly grips onto her finger and stops screaming.

"I think he looks like a Lucas."

"Lucas," Scarlett breathes, looking up at me. "I like it."

"Me, too."

"Let's do it."

"Hi, Lucas." Chloe smiles and rubs a finger over his tiny knuckles. "My name is Chloe, and I'm going to be the best big sister. I've always wanted a little brother, and I know I'm a lot older than you, but I promise I'll always be here for you."

I can't help it, I break down and bawl like a baby, and Scarlett reaches for my hand.

"They're perfect together, Tuck. We have two perfect kids."

"We're all done, who wants him first?" the nurse says, picking up our son. He's swaddled in a blanket, and I look at Scarlett, who looks at Chloe.

Scarlett has had a lot of concerns about how Chloe would feel after the birth of our baby. It's important to her that Chloe doesn't feel left out or as though we love him more. Chloe assures us that she's fine and just excited for the baby, but I know it weighs heavily on Scarlett's mind.

"Do you want to hold him first, Chloe?" Scarlett asks.

Chloe's eyes widen. They brim with tears and happiness. "Really?"

Scarlett nods. "Go ahead."

Chloe situates herself on the bed beside Scarlett, and the nurse gently places Lucas into her arms. With an arm around Chloe's shoulder, Scarlett coos at our baby boy, and all I can do is stare at my family in awe.

"I love you, Chloe," Scarlett says, brushing a strand of hair from Chloe's forehead. "You will always be my firstborn. My sweet baby girl, even though you weren't so little when you came into my life."

"And I wasn't very sweet," Chloe says, smiling.

"You've always been sweet, and I love you very much. You know that, right?"

"I know," Chloe whispers. "I love you, too."

Scarlett wipes a tear from her cheek and reaches for my hand. "Come on, Daddy, come meet your son."

It seems like so long since Chloe was a baby. She's so big now, and Lucas is so tiny.

I cuddle in close to my wife and two children.

"Look," Chloe says, laughing. "I think he's smiling."

"It could be gas. You used to make that face right before you loaded your pants."

We all laugh.

Lucas yawns and then starts to root on Chloe.

"Someone is hungry," I say, reaching for our son.

"I'll step out." Chloe kisses Lucas on the head and then hugs Scarlett.

"Tell Grandma, Grandpa, and Rick that they can come in as soon as she's done feeding him," I say.

"I will."

Chloe slips out of the room, and I cuddle Lucas while Scarlett pulls down her gown. I hand her our son. She cradles him to her chest like a pro, and he fusses around at her breast for a couple of seconds before finally latching on.

It's such a beautiful sight—one that I never got to experience with Chloe.

"You're so beautiful, sweetheart."

Scarlett looks at me. "I'm a hot mess."

"You're my hot mess." I kiss her forehead and then stroke her cheek and turn her face to mine for a sweet, soft kiss. "I love you more than you'll ever know."

She smiles against my lips. "I think I have a pretty good idea."

THE END

ALSO BY K.L. GRAYSON

Did you enjoy Already Gone? Want to know when my next book is coming out? Sign up for my **newsletter** (12 newsletters or less per year) OR sign up for my **new release alert** (you'll only be notified when a new release is available)

UP NEXT (Available for preorder):

The Boyfriend Blog

A Touch of Fate Series

(Contemporary Romance)

Where We Belong

Pretty Pink Ribbons

On Solid Ground

Live Without Regret

Dirty Dicks Series (Contemporary Romance)

Crazy Sexy Love

Crazy Hot Love

Crazy Stupid Love

Crazy Imperfect Love

Crazy Beautiful Love

Single Titles

Wait For Me

Stay With Me

A Lover's Lament

The Truth About Lennon

<u>Black</u>

<u>Short Stories FREE in KU</u>

<u>Double Score</u>

<u>Nice Until Proven Naughty</u>

<u>www.KLGrayson.com</u>

Easy Kisses

Easy Magic

Easy Fortune

Easy Nights

The With Me In Seattle Series:

Come Away With Me

Under the Mistletoe With Me

Fight With Me

Play With Me

Rock With Me

Safe With Me

Tied With Me

Burn With Me

Breathe With Me

Forever With Me

Stay With Me

Indulge With Me

Love With Me

Dance With Me

The Love Under the Big Sky Series:

Loving Cara

Seducing Lauren

Falling For Jillian

Saving Grace

From 1001 Dark Nights:

Easy With You

Easy For Keeps

No Reservations

Made in the
USA
Middletown, DE